I0719281

A TALE OF GEOMETRY

A TALE OF GEOMETRY

OLIVERA JELKIC

Globland Books

A wide variety of witches, dragons and bogeymen inhabit our world. Generally speaking, people fear the unknown. Geometry is certainly one that "spoils children's fun". But this disappears once they get to know each other, once children have peered through the keyhole and seen that geometry consists of an assortment of good-natured creatures who also fear the unknown. They fear lack of knowledge: children's lack of knowledge that shatters and distorts them, crosses them out and crumples them up. These are creatures who dread every quiz, every test, terrified of what they'll resemble afterward and what injuries they'll sustain.

Until these two worlds get to know each other, fear will prevail. So let's peer together into that unknown, into that bogeyman called "geometry". You might just like it and you might fall in love with it, and never want to be separated again.

THE GEOMETRY CLASSROOM

1.

At the end of the last class, the children got their book bags ready. When the bell rang, they crowded through the doors and in a few minutes the classrooms were empty. Behind them they left broken chalk, wet sponges, scribbled blackboards, unused cheat sheets, forgotten pencils. There was also an umbrella that had been hanging there for years. Who knows who forgot it and when.

The geometry classroom was in total chaos. Just like after a battle. Actually, after a test. Scattered around were papers, rulers, lopsided circles, lots of polygons, and (attempted) cones. The Pyramid of Cheops. Nooo. An ordinary pyramid. The Pyramid of Cheops fell out of someone's history reader, although there is a conspiracy theory that the history teacher, known as "Cheops" to the children, had intentionally left it there so the geometry teacher, Miss Sofia, known as "Miss Symmetry", would think of him.

In any case, the "situation on the ground" made it clear that an A in geometry would not soon show its face.

***

The cleaning lady entered the classroom. The children had different names for her, since she was always hounding them and bringing them into line. They considered her a real nuisance, and even a tyrant. Her name was Lenka, but they most often called her "Boss" owing to her extremely dictatorial attitude toward them. Actually, no one was let off the hook, not even the teachers.

She tried to corner at least one student every time so she could give them a lesson on hygiene and order in the classroom. The time she spent "lecturing" was enough to clean two classrooms, but she really enjoyed this role.

"Well, now you're going to clean all of this by yourself," she said to Andrew who was the last to leave the classroom.

"Why me? I didn't do all that by myself. Plus..."

"Don't give me that runaround! All you do is make a mess and break these poor triangles," she replied.

"Triangles? But that's not a triangle, it's a protractor," said Andrew.

"Makes no difference. You break one and the other. You break whatever you touch. But let me ask you something, and you look me straight in the eyes and tell me the truth: What're you secretly planning over there by the playground? I see you all in a group! Don't let me hear that you're up to some rabblerousing, you'll have me to deal with."

"What rabblerousing... what's that, rabblerousing? We don't even know what that is," stuttered Andrew.

"Don't you play Mr. Nice Guy with me! I know you kids. You're all wiseacres."

"What's a 'wiseacre'? We're just kids, and not that..." said Andrew.

"You're splitting hairs again. Just stand there. Don't move! I want to ask you one more thing and I expect you to tell me the truth!"

"That's what I'm doing, telling the truth," said Andrew weakly.

"Who's been making a mess in the classroom at night? Huh? You little rowdy! Who's been creating havoc at night in the dark, right here in the geometry classroom? Come on, kiddo, let's hear you!"

"At night? Who would come to school at night? We get enough of school during the day. No one's crazy enough to come to school at night to study," he said, quite confused by the question.

"Don't you beat around the bush with me! I've been setting traps for you, but haven't caught you yet. Well, not for long! Boss will catch you. Go ahead and clown around. I'll tie your ears into a bow!" she threatened.

As they talked, Andrew kept trying to reach the door and escape, but the cleaning lady cut him off, so they almost ran around the classroom.

"I know you better than you know yourselves! I'll straighten you all out! Keep up with that secret whispering. I took care of that principal, the one who left, and the one before him, and the school psychologist as well. I lay down the law for them! Do you hear what Lenka's saying? When you talk to me you have to stand still and not beat around the bush!"

Andrew barely escaped her claws. His friends were already waiting behind the school playground.

"The cleaning lady again? When are we going to get free of her?" said Una.

"Never. She'll keep trying to bring things to order even when she retires," concluded Katarina.

"Just imagine, guys, she asked me which one of us was making a mess in the geometry classroom at night. Hey, at night! Who's going to go to school at night? This daytime stuff is already too much for me," said Andrew.

"At night?!" they said in unison, looking at each other in amazement.

"Really, who'd go into the geometry classroom at night?"

"She must have made it up," concluded Una.

"She's not exactly... from this planet... you know what I mean, but I don't think she makes things up," said Andrew.

"It's certainly intriguing. Can we shadow who enters the school at night?" proposed Una.

"Detective problems are really exciting," said Katarina.

2.

Mr. Theodore, the teacher known as "Mr. Pythagoras" and Miss Sofia, known affectionately by the children as "Miss Symmetry", worked in opposite school sessions and shared the same classroom. They taught mathematics, but both of them were in love with *Her Highness Geometry*.

They only met at the end of the first session when students from the second session entered the classrooms. Mr. Theodore waited eagerly for the bell to ring, more excited than any of the children.

No, he was not bored by the class. On the contrary. geometry was his great love, but even greater was his love for the geometry teacher – Miss Symmetry.

But please don't tell a soul. Shhhh.

That day she entered the classroom a bit before the class ended. She apologized politely to her colleague for interrupting his class.

He stood up like a student called on by the teacher to answer a question and get a better grade.

"Excuse me for disturbing you. I just wanted to ask whether you have anyone for the geometry competition."

"Thank you for thinking of our class. Yes, many here love geometry: Cindy, Pro, Sissy, Obtuse and his brother Obtusely, then there's Alfonso, Bette, Tiago, and some others."

The students were perplexed. Those names didn't belong to any of them and the teacher had mentioned almost an entire class.

"Wonderful, please make a list and leave it on the desk and we'll invite them to the school competition," said Miss Symmetry. She said goodbye politely and left the classroom. Mr. Pythagoras was still standing like a student, waiting for someone to tell him to sit down.

The bell rang signaling the end of the class. It was the favorite bell of the dozen that rang during the session.

The students ran out of the geometry classroom, leaving their teacher still dazed by his encounter with Miss Symmetry. As he packed his things into his bag, everything kept slipping out of his hands.

Everyone had already left the classroom and the next session would soon enter. He picked up his bag and went out.

Several minutes later the second session entered the classroom. Miss Symmetry put the roll book on the desk.

"Monitor! Whoever is the monitor today, please wipe the blackboard..."

Then she looked at Mr. Pythagoras' open drawer. It was always locked and she suspected that a great secret was hidden inside. She pulled the drawer open all the way so no one else could see, and there inside was a large format notebook entitled:

PYTHAGORAS' PHANTASMAGORY
A Tale of Geometry

Miss Symmetry was fascinated by the title. She sat there, ready to close the drawer immediately should her colleague Mr. Pythagoras come back to lock it or take the manuscript.

She realized she was doing something she shouldn't, but curiosity got the best of her.

"Children, please go over the last lesson and do this problem, then we'll continue with the class. Write this down: 'The sum of two angles with parallel sides is 346'. Determine the size of these angles if:

(a) one angle is seven times greater than the other,

(b) one angle is 62° greater than the other.

There's something urgent I have to attend to," she said, so she could look at the manuscript without being disturbed. She picked it up and started to read:

It was not so long ago, in a land called Geometry, a great and beautiful land in the center of the huge Archipelago of Mathematics. Its inhabitants were happy, but very measured, precise and calculated. Order and rules were followed and they strictly adhered to the laws of Geometry.

But the ground often shook, mixing everything up, turning everything upside down, making it hard to tell who was from which island of this rambling archipelago.

Actually, these were not earthquakes, but typhoons called Tests. It was common knowledge that they came at regular and irregular intervals, announced and unannounced, and no one could avoid them. Excuses didn't work. It didn't even help if: "I spent the whole night stuck in the elevator" or "my great-aunt died" (for the seventh time), or "we had a power outage, so I couldn't do my homework". No excuses.

If you managed somehow to avoid one, another would be waiting just around the corner. You never knew when a typhoon-test would pop up and from which field. All you knew was that it usually left a wasteland behind it.

When it was all over, the land of Geometry was restored. Its inhabitants cleaned the streets, fixed up the parks and once again it became the most orderly land in the world. Once again it was a real pleasure to live there.

The land of Geometry has the shape of a regular circle. A straight street called Radius goes from the center toward the seashore. There you will find a multitude of precisely bordered squares.

Polygon Square is celebrated. It is divided into several smaller squares: Triangular Square, Pentagon Square, Octagon Square.

Pythagoras Square certainly has the most visitors. It has a monument dedicated to Triangle containing the following theorem: "the square of the length of the hypotenuse equals the sum of the squares of the lengths of the other two sides".

In the very center of Geometry there is a Roundabout. It has a monument dedicated to Point.

Why Point? Hmm, I'm sure you wonder.

***

"Teacher, I finished the problem," said Una.

"Wonderful. You're always first. Let's wait for the others to finish," said Miss Symmetry, giving herself a few more minutes to go back to the text in Mr. Pythagoras' notebook.

"What an interesting way to look at geometry," she thought. "Hmm. I know he has nice eyes, but who would have thought my colleague Theodore has such a gift for literature and such imagination, that's something I never would have suspected."

Almost no one knew his real name. If someone asked for Theodore Sage, it's unlikely that anyone would remember. They simply called him Mr. Pythagoras. Teacher Pythagoras.

Just then Miss Symmetry heard footsteps heading toward the classroom. She closed the notebook quickly and put it back in the drawer.

He appeared at the door. Theodore Sage. Mr. Pythagoras. When he saw Sofia, his eyes lit up. She smiled, a little bewildered and said hello.

"Did you forget something?"

"Me? No. I mean – yes. Actually – no. I mean... I forgot some papers," said Theodore. "Actually, a notebook where I write... what I need to buy at the market."

He sighed several times, took his manuscript out of the drawer and left the classroom.

He was flustered and found refuge in the school library's reading room. She was in his thoughts. Sofia. Miss Symmetry. But he didn't dare tell her his feelings. He had the jitters, like students before a geometry test.

Quite a few were in love with Miss Symmetry. It can't be said that this didn't bother him. It bothered him. A lot. He was very jealous, but he hid it, considering jealousy a weakness and a very bad trait, which was certainly correct.

He was primarily jealous of the history teacher, particularly when he saw the picture of the Pyramid of Cheops that had made its way into the geometry classroom as though it belonged there.

In addition, he was jealous of someone else, but he wouldn't admit it to save his life. The protractor. Yes, yes. Old Protractor Pro was certainly in love with Miss Symmetry. And she might be in love with him too, otherwise why would she periodically carry him around in her purse and not let him out of her sight?

Theodore put the book manuscript on a table and started reading for the umpteenth time, writing new sentences and even new paragraphs. He corrected mistakes with a red pencil, just like on a test. No matter how many times he read it, he still found little typos or mistakes in style, or felt the need to add something. Of course, he wanted the book to be perfect.

* * *

With regard to the book, Theodore had a secret. He liked to sit in the geometry classroom when no one was there and write in peace.

It's not certain whether he actually wrote his book in peace, since no one saw what he did at night.

And so one evening he was sitting in the classroom, writing. Even now it's not quite certain whether it really happened or not. He might have been drowsy or else some magic was involved, but he heard the geometric forms talking.

He never said a word to anyone about it. It was his deepest secret.

Actually, that was how he started writing the book, when he was correcting test papers in the classroom. After everyone left, he stayed alone, locked in the school.

He didn't make anything up. Everything he wrote was true.

Chapter One

CONCENTRIC CIRCLE CINDY

Once upon a time there was a circle named Cindy. She was not an ordinary circle, but a concentric circle, considered among circles to be a higher class, nobility, so to speak.

She was surrounded by a multitude of triangles, segments, ellipses, squares, trapezoids, but they were not as important as Cindy, who thought they existed for the sole purpose of admiring her.

Nevertheless, in spite of so much company, Cindy was very bored. It might be said that Cindy was lonely in the middle of that crowd. Yes. Most lonely people live in big cities. It was like that in Geometry too.

She was constantly spinning in a circle, smoothing her petticoat and admiring it. That was her only job during the day. She wouldn't allow anyone to touch her. But when night fell, Cindy had a big problem: she couldn't sleep because of her petticoat, so she dozed standing up. That's why she often wakened without a good night's sleep and was on edge. No one held this against her, since she was everyone's favorite, except for those who didn't consider her their favorite at all.

It's true that Cindy was the prettiest in all of fifth grade geometry. She was completely aware of this even before, but after they took her picture for the cover of *Geometry Workbook*, no one was Cindy's equal anymore.

Indeed, Cindy was not the only one on that cover. There were some triangles, segments, radiuses, straight and of curvature; there were klutzy trapezoids and Fanny Fan who happened to be visiting Trapezoid Tiago; there were penta-grams and octagrams and two kilograms that were put there on purpose to give geometry some weight. But they were all overshadowed by beautiful Concentric Circle Cindy. She was the perfection of geometry.

Many admired her, but some were envious. Actually, cir-cles envied her the most.

Ordinary, single circles did not have the courage to envy her. They adored her and were proud of her.

"That's Cindy, our sister. She's not our sibling, rather our first cousin, but we love her just like a sibling," they said.

They put her picture on the wall of their study and boasted that she was their cousin from Hollywood. When they were alone, they would daydream and try to concen-trate like Cindy and become concentric circles.

Some evil tongues claimed that Cindy was conceited, her nose in the air, but this was only conjecture since Cindy's nose could not be seen from the dense succession of con-centric circles that comprised her beautiful petticoat.

"Why are you spinning so much? You'll get dizzy," Ellie Ellipse said to her.

Cindy stopped, raised her petticoat and looked down. When she saw Ellie Ellipse staring at her, Cindy took a step back.

"Oh, who flattened you like that?" screamed Cindy.

"Excuse me?! What do you mean? What's your objection?" replied Ellie sharply.

"No, nothing. Does it hurt?" continued Cindy.

"Does it hurt? Does what hurt?" said Ellie Ellipse, baffled.

"The fact that someone flattened you," repeated Cindy.

"You're talking nonsense, and you want to advance to sixth grade," replied Ellie.

"Poor thing. You must have been through a lot of hard tests. Battles and wars. You might even have taken a makeup test, since you're so drawn out," said Cindy.

"Maybe I did take a makeup test, but you won't get that chance. You're going to repeat fifth grade one hundred times!" said Ellie Ellipse.

"Me? It's not very nice for a veteran of so many wars to talk nonsense and not speak the truth!" replied Cindy in her defense.

"Maybe I am a veteran of many wars, but you aren't included in the sixth grade curriculum. You're an ordinary two-dimensional flat geometric shape and only three-dimensional geometric figures go to sixth grade."

Cindy couldn't believe it. Until then she'd been convinced that she would be part of all the geometry textbooks from fifth grade to the end of university studies, and even beyond, if there was anything beyond.

Cindy almost fainted at this bad news. Actually, she couldn't even fall because of her petticoat. So she started crying at the top of her lungs and no one could calm her down. They all gathered around, wanting to console her.

The triangles came first. They venerated her as though she were a princess. So they just looked at her silently, with compassion, as Cindy bawled her eyes out.

After a while, Obtuse Triangle Obtuse spoke up.

"Concentric Circle Cindy, why are you crying? I won't advance to sixth grade either, but I'm not crying."

"You? You're not even for fifth grade, you're so obtuse! Why should I be in the same book as you?" said Cindy, crying even harder.

The other triangles pushed Obtuse behind them, as though wanting to hide the shame and embarrassment they felt because of his dull-witted comment.

One even boxed him on the ears and sent him into a corner.

"What did I do wrong?" said Obtuse. "I didn't tell a lie. I really will repeat fifth grade. You won't be alone, beautiful Cindy. My brother Obtusely will also repeat. And it's not our first time. We repeat fifth grade as a family and don't get upset. We really like it here. We're all together, we hang out, and because we know we'll repeat, no one gets mad. Don't cry, beautiful Cindy, you'll smudge your petticoat..."

As he said this, Right-Angled Triangle came up and closed his mouth, so he couldn't even finish his sentence.

When he had silenced Obtuse, he went up to Cindy.

"Cindy, sweet queen," he said and didn't know what to say next. He repeated this several times.

Cindy quieted down a little, expecting him to continue, but when she saw that he didn't know what else to say, she burst out crying even harder.

"You phony little triangle! You just pretend to be right-angled! You're obtuse too! Where's that Protractor Pro! He should come at once and measure you!"

When the triangle heard the name Protractor Pro, he ran as fast as he could and hid in a dark corner.

Cindy kept crying, more by force of habit, and the other triangles fell silent, until she got tired of entertaining them like that.

"What's wrong? What are you looking at? Like you've never seen me before. Like you won't repeat fifth grade!? I don't know how you ever got to fifth grade, all angular like that! You can't even roll like normal people. Just see how I can," said Cindy and spun in a circle as hard as she could as her skirt of a thousand circles started gently rolling.

Everyone blinked and sighed, and one trapezoid got dizzy and fainted.

A gasp escaped from a little square. A large pentagram looked at him sternly and said:

"What're you huffing about, you little square kid. If someone should huff, it's me!"

"Why you?" asked an isosceles triangle.

"Because they call me Pentagram Star! Isn't that enough. I'm the only one who would suit a circle like Cindy."

"Hey, wait a minute! What's that I hear? Why you? Cindy and I would make the most wonderful couple in Andalusia," said Trapezoid Tiago.

"Do my ears deceive me?" asked Tiago's Fanny Fan, looking at him darkly. Trapezoid Tiago bowed his head and said:

"You didn't hear well.... darling."

"That's better already. Let's go back to our Andalusia where such vanity doesn't exist!" replied Fanny, grabbing her Tiago's hand to take him home.

"Hmm, vain! I'm not Vain! I'm Super Vain!" exclaimed Cindy.

Then she spun even faster, more out of rage for having to repeat the year than from the satisfaction she got at having them watch her and admire her.

Right then, quite by chance, Protractor Pro appeared – in person. He was the terror of Geometry, the supreme chief who had the last word.

"What happened? What's going on here? Is someone causing disorder?" he asked sternly. "That cannot be allowed! There must be order in Geometry!"

Everyone fell silent. Not a sound was heard. Cindy was still spinning, but slower and slower, and then she stopped completely.

Protractor Pro frowned and said:

"I can tell you're hiding something from me. Alright, everyone line up so Uncle Pro can measure you a little."

"There's no need. You measured us yesterday," said Right-Angled Triangle.

"That was yesterday. Let's see how things stand today," continued Protractor Pro. "First you, the grumbler. Let's see. Give me that acute angle to measure. Aha. Forty-five degrees."

"There, you see," replied Right-Angled Triangle.

"Let's see the next one! Forty-four!" he shouted in amazement.

"What?!" exclaimed the others.

"Ninety-one!" continued Pro, measuring the third angle that was supposed to be ninety degrees, a right angle.

"Haha!" said Cindy. "I knew he was a phony. He just pretended to be right-angled and actually he's obtuse!"

Triangle was perplexed, as though not knowing what had happened to him.

"I have to admit, brothers, "he said.

"Whose brother are you, obtuse like that? You're actually Obtuse and Obtusely's first cousin, but you're hiding it," shouted someone from the crowd.

"Listen to me, please," continued Triangle, former right-angled and now obtuse-angled.

"Listen to him," added Zaza Circle, who had been ready to console him for some time and now recognized her chance.

"I have to admit, I had a serious mishap. I was in a test with a boy who got a D, and came out of it like an invalid. Otherwise, I was born right-angled, but, there you have it, life is a battle. I came out with one shorter side."

"Poor little triangle!" said Zaza Circle and circumscribed him with her circle as best she could. Then they went home together so the others wouldn't make fun of him.

Nevertheless, one circle started laughing out loud.

"Haha! What a couple. He's obtuse and she acts like a circle, but she's really an ellipse. Measure her, Uncle Pro, and you'll see she's a phony too," she said.

"Why don't you come over here so Uncle Protractor can measure you a little. You're the loudmouth here."

"Why me?" said the noisy circle in surprise.

"Just because. You look a little suspicious," added Pro and started measuring her.

"Of course. I've got a sharp eye. Three hundred fifty-nine degrees and three minutes. Wretched girl, where did you tramp around and lose fifty-seven minutes?" concluded Pro.

"That's impossible!" she cried.

"Do you doubt me and my precision?" asked Protractor Pro.

"It's not true that I lost something. Here, let the others look. What am I missing? Nothing!"

"Nothing?" continued Pro. "You're not a circle at all. You don't exist at all. Come on, tell me which geometric shape has three hundred fifty-nine degrees and three minutes? Which one?"

No one spoke, and Pro continued as though lecturing in class:

"Of course, everyone can see there is none."

"That's not true!" said the circle angrily. "I'm going to slam you with a radius! You're not calibrated! See how old you are! Your numbers have worn off!" she said and burst into tears.

"Why don't you measure Cindy? You never measure her. You only measure us, you're only suspicious of us," shouted a double circle at Protractor Pro.

"Cindy? Well, I can't measure Cindy," he replied, his eyes turning melancholy.

"Why not?" they all asked in unison.

"I can't. Her mother forbid me from measuring her. She's afraid someone will injure her," replied Pro.

"Who's her mother, anyway?" asked an inquisitive circle.

"Why is it veiled in secrecy?" asked a radius.

"Her mother? Well, her mother is a lady," replied Protractor Pro.

"Where did you meet her?" asked a curious square of the hypotenuse.

Pro sat on Segment AB lying there like a bench and leaned an arm against the old square known as Artemius. He sighed deeply several times, looked into the distance and started speaking softly:

"I haven't told anyone before. Maybe because no one ever asked me. I'm the oldest here. When I came, there was no one here. 'Tabula rasa' as the old Latins say."

"What does that mean in our Geometry language?" asked Cone Joan.

"It means 'blank slate'. The papers were blank and clean. The notebooks were new, everything rustled. And then She came."

"She?" they asked in unison.

"She. Miss Symmetry. As pretty as a pixie, gentle and smiling," said Pro wistfully.

"What? Miss Symmetry is her mother? The geometry teacher?" they concluded.

"I remember back when I was a young protractor, we were all in love with her. A ruler snapped from too much love. They say she broke a protractor's heart before me, and that's when I joined the service. We all loved her and waited for her geometry class.

"Then one day a man came to school to teach geometry."

"Mr. Pythagoras?" they said in surprise.

"Theodor Sage, known as Mr. Pythagoras. You're right. I remember when he entered the classroom, I must admit he was handsome, young, tall and blond. But a little confused. He extended his hand to Miss Symmetry. She smiled.

'Welcome, colleague,' she said in her gentle voice.

"He handed her a small package. She unwrapped it and placed a thin nickel-plated compass on the desk. It was so shiny that we couldn't look at it without sunglasses.

"Miss Symmetry picked it up and caressed it gently. I must admit that we were all quite jealous of that new Compass, and yet we knew that compared to him, so slim and graceful, we didn't stand a chance.

"Mr. Pythagoras put a large, clean white sheet of paper on the desk. This was a challenge for all of us. A competition began at once in drawing various triangles, quadrilaterals, trapezoids. We raced to see who could draw the most, the best, the prettiest. When we had shown what we knew how to do, Conrad Compass rose, guided by Miss Symmetry's hand, and took several energetic steps.

"Believe it or not, we heard a fanfare right then. Conrad Compass walked with an officer's stride and graceful stature. He stood in the middle of the paper. Everyone fell silent. He turned toward the teachers and saluted, then thrust his sharp tip into the paper and started turning virtuously in a circle, making pirouettes, leaving beautiful concentric circles on the paper. The thunderous sound of "The Blue Danube" Viennese waltz was suddenly heard: pam-pam, pam-pam, pam-pam, pam-pam…

"We all stared fixedly. He looked like a dancing silver whirlwind. Miss Symmetry did not hide her love. We had the impression that she was dancing with him, they had merged into one, into a silver contour, a three-quarter tact, a harmony, a wave on the Danube.

"When the music stopped, Conrad Compass bowed, kissed his darling's hand and moved aside.

"In the middle of the paper stood their masterpiece. It was She. Concentric Circle Cindy."

Protractor Pro finished his romantic story. A tear formed in the corner of his eye. He stared into the distance a little while longer.

Some of them took advantage of this and hid in a safe place, so he couldn't measure them.

Ellie Ellipse broke the silence.

"Can you imagine, Miss Symmetry! So what if her mother is the geometry teacher? So what! Cindy still can't advance to sixth grade! She can't and that's final!"

Cindy burst into tears again and Protractor Pro said:

"Wait a minute, something's happening here?! Who's going to explain it to me?"

"Ellie Ellipse claims that Cindy has to repeat fifth grade because she's not included in the curriculum for sixth grade," explained Acute Angle Spike.

"Aha, now I get it! That's why Cindy is crying!" concluded Pro, and said, "Cindy, don't shed tears in vain. It's true that geometric bodies are taught in sixth grade, but please tell me, how can you draw a cone without a circle? How can you make a cube without a square? How can you make a sphere without a radius? How can you?

"Of course you can't. The only thing I'm not sure of is the ellipse. I think it's a bit different with them," said Pro and winked, more to himself.

Everyone seemed to be happy with this explanation, except Ellie Ellipse. She opened her jaw very wide, and just when they all thought she would devour them, she started screaming in anger. Then she turned and slid down a ray to infinity.

***

Mr. Pythagoras closed his eyes. He heard the sounds of a waltz in his head. Before him was the image of Miss Symmetry. He hoped that she would find out about his feelings through the book. That would certainly be easier than standing before her and saying:

I love you, dear Sofia.

He could barely wait to see her in the geometry class-room when the sessions changed. He liked it best when he had the fifth class in the first session and she had the first class in the second session. He was more eager than the children for the final bell to ring, but tried to hide his impatience.

Whenever they met, he became so flustered that he inevitably dropped a triangle or ruler on the floor. He regularly appeared muddle-headed and distracted, and he reproached himself, since he knew she noticed his awkwardness.

"You're such a bungler," he would say to himself whenever this happened. Miss Symmetry would help him pick up his scattered drawing equipment, the workbooks that fell on the floor, his bag with odds and ends falling out of it. She would smile at him every time as though it was nothing terrible.

"That happens to everyone," she would say in a soft voice.

"Yes, it happens to everyone, of course," he would think, "but it only happens to me every time. When will it ever happen that it doesn't happen to me?" he asked himself. "When will I muster the courage to go up to her, without anything falling out of my hands?" he wondered.

He noticed a decrease in his insecurity when he started to write. So he lost no time and wrote every day, or rather wrote every night whenever he managed to sneak into the geometry room without being noticed.

His book grew and with it his hopes that the book would help him tell her everything he wanted to, without dropping his geometry equipment on the floor.

And so one evening when the janitor known as Boss left the room and took the garbage to the dumpster, Mr. Pythagoras sneaked back into the classroom. He did not turn on the light until he heard the school gate click shut. This was a sure sign that Boss had gone home and would not return until morning.

No one could take issue with her, since she was louder and more persistent than anyone. She took matters into her own hands and tried to create order. If she ever succeeded, she would have been out of a job. But this never crossed her mind. On closer inspection, she didn't even expect the children to learn to be orderly. She simply enjoyed lecturing them about it.

Mr. Pythagoras waited a little longer, just long enough for Boss to disappear around the corner on her infamous bike, and then headed to turn on the light.

Just when he got to the light switch, he heard voices in the classroom. Moonlight bathed the school desks, making other light almost unnecessary. He realized that something was happening. Instead of turning on the light, he picked up a pen and continued to record the classroom's adventures.

Chapter Two

ASINUS

Everything seemed quite peaceful. It looked like they were all sleeping after the final exam that had passed that day like a typhoon with the same aftermath a typhoon would leave on a far-off Pacific island.

A sharp eye would not be able to see anything in the dark, but a sharp ear? Well, that's another thing. A sharp ear would hear moaning, screaming and cries for help.

Mr. Pythagoras sat at the teacher's desk and closed his eyes. He started sinking into his fantasies, going deeper and deeper until the parallel world of geometric figures appeared before him.

And then, first as though through a mist, and then quite clearly, he saw Miss Symmetry enter the classroom, turn on the desk lamp, and put the children's workbooks on the desk from which sighs, screams and moaning could be heard.

He could see her clearly, but she could not see him. This is often a great advantage. He could gaze at her to his heart's content.

Miss Symmetry opened the workbooks and arranged them on the teacher's desk. What a sight she had to see: it was just like a battlefield after a battle. There were broken sides, drawn out circles, scattered degrees and minutes, their owners unknown; there were shattered radiuses and some tangled lines. They moaned as they took care of their wounds.

Miss Symmetry grabbed her head in her hands when she saw what awaited her.

"My poor little triangles. It must have really hurt," she said and picked up a splint to set a fracture. It was not a real medical splint, but a small ruler. Protractor Pro was there too, since nothing fared well without him, and situations like this were particularly challenging. He was some sort of policeman, although he didn't wear a uniform except on formal occasions.

Then Miss Symmetry took a pencil and tried to treat their injuries. Just as on every battlefield, the blood was knee deep, so the pencil turned red and left behind a trace that made one's hair stand on end. This treating the wounded lasted and lasted.

When the work was done, Miss Symmetry closed the workbooks, turned off the light and left the classroom.

The wounded were still preoccupied with their injuries and a moan would be heard periodically, just as a formality, out of habit.

After a while, Logarithm spoke up from the margin.

"That's enough wailing! Why are you moaning when you've all been repaired? Look at yourselves. You're all just like new. Almost like new."

They looked first at him, blinking their eyes, clearly bewildered by his presence, and then looked at their injuries.

Indeed, they were all healed. Where a side had been missing there was now a new red side, made to order.

"Hey, kids, we really are just like new! Everything's alright!" said a triangle.

"Will you look at that, my radius is back where it belongs!" added a circle.

"Why am I not tangent to anyone?" asked Tina Tangent who had been crossed out and pushed aside.

"Poor thing, so alone," replied tall and handsome Sine from the fifth problem.

As soon as he spoke, Mrs. Sine Wave, better known as Sissy, cleared her throat pointedly behind his back.

"Oh, sorry, Sissy, I thought... actually I wasn't thinking," he said, embarrassed.

"Look, he's retreated," said Christy Chord. "You can see his wife's jealous. She follows him like a shadow, he can't even move without her being aware. She often turns red from jealousy. There, now she's turned red."

Christy Chord was hurt at Sissy's reaction, since she too was alone and had been crossed out in red as unnecessary in the problem.

"But, he spoke to me first. How can I put it, he took notice of me!" explained Tina Tangent. "He's actually not at all my type. I wouldn't be tangent to him if he was the last one in the world. Just look at him..."

Sissy Sine Wave cleared her throat again and joined the conversation.

"What's that you say? He took notice of you? Haha! He's had enough of those stiff, thin and powdered ones that just stick onto those who like it and those who don't. Well, you see, he doesn't like it! Remember that! He likes round ones, like me!" said Sissy, taking her Sine by the arm.

And then she added:

"I know about you guys who are crossed out and set aside. You just hunt around for someone to be their tangent. The graduation ball is approaching and you need a partner to dance with! It's the same every year. Why didn't you attend to it earlier? In any case, here's this Cosine. He's alone. He just pushes in next to my husband. Where there's one, there's the other. Like Siamese twins. He won't let me live. Why doesn't someone stick onto him?"

"Someone has!" said Cosine.

"What! That's impossible! Congratulations," said Sissy Sine Wave.

"Thanks for nothing," replied Cosine.

"For nothing?! Now I suppose you'll unhitch from my husband, Mr. Sine."

"I'd rather this guy unhitched from me. He gets on my nerves. He brays all the time!" explained Cosine.

"Brays? No one brays here except after a hard test. Even then, they mostly moan, not bray. Someone who gets an F might bray a little, but they cry more than bray."

"Brays! Who's the guy who brays?" asked the others.

"He's got big ears. He says his name is Asinus and I'm his twin brother. Like Cosine and Asinus," explained Cosine.

"Asinus! Never heard of him. Does anyone know him?" asked Sine.

"I know him," said Logarithm. "But he's not from geometry. He wandered out of first year high school Latin and couldn't advance to the next grade, because he's..."

"Because he's?" asked the others in unison.

"Because he's..."

"Because he's?"

"Because he's... a donkey," explained Logarithm.

"A donkey?!" said everyone in unison. "What's a donkey doing in geometry?"

"Let's get rid of him as soon as we can, before someone finds out. What a disgrace!" said a circle.

"How shameful, I hope no one from arithmetic finds out we breed donkeys! They always compete with us over who's smarter," said a triangle.

"Give me that radius! I'll chase him away," volunteered Trapezoid Tiago.

"What?! Darling, you can't chase a donkey! What if someone heard us in Andalusia? We'll be a laughingstock," said Tiago's Fanny Fan.

"You're a toreador, darling. You fight dangerous bulls. You're not some Sancho Panza on a donkey," she said and waved her fan several times to show how classy she was.

"But someone has to get rid of him," said Sissy Sine Wave.

"Well, how about Mr. Sine. He's a... real man," said Christy Chord.

"Hmm, why him?" interjected Sissy. "Let the one he's attached to get rid of him. As far as I'm concerned, he can leave along with him. Then he won't attach onto my husband anymore. What's wrong with that? Cosine and Asinus. It has a ring to it!" she said cynically.

"Hmm, Sine and Asinus also has a ring. Like twins. You're all fishy to me. What do you mean, first year high school Latin. Do you know how far away that is? He had to cross half the world to get to fifth grade geometry," said Ellie Ellipse.

"Listen here, girl, you leave my husband alone. You're not immune either. This unwelcome citizen of Geometry could attach onto you too. 'Persona non grata', as some... some foreigners say!" replied Sissy.

"Latins, dear Sissy, Latins. Hmm, you seem fishy to me," noted Ellie Ellipse.

When Cosine heard all of this, he bowed his head and said:

"Alright, stop bickering. I'll get rid of him. Give me that radius and I'll threaten him with it."

He took the radius in both hands and went in search of Asinus to chase him out of Geometry, since in the meantime he had gotten lost like a donkey in the mist.

Cosine searched everywhere, but there was no sign of him. The others searched too. They peered into problems, looked under every polygon, even behind the pentagon who put on airs and did not allow anyone to get near him.

They looked for him everywhere and Cosine finally came across a Spot, who was not a welcome sight in Geometry. They even called him names: Stain, Scribble, and even Blot.

Cosine was about to go back, since he didn't want to rub shoulders with just anyone or be seen with that Spot, when Spot said:

"Are you looking for that crazy donkey?"

"How do you know?"

"Well, you're carrying that hoe, who else would you be looking for?"

"It's not a hoe. It's my colleague – Radius, except that he's versatile and can be used for various purposes."

"Aha, I know. He took a martial arts course."

"That's it. He knows how to fight and if you don't stop talking I'll show you right this instant."

"You know what, Cosine, you show that to someone else, and that first cousin of yours..."

"Who's my first cousin? I don't have any first cousin," said Cosine angrily.

"Asinus!?"

"Him? How can he be my first cousin? He wandered out of first year high school, from the Latin class."

"I don't know if he went wandering, but he's certainly not from here. That I can believe. He told me he was your first cousin."

"Just wait until I catch him! That bad-mannered donkey's lying!" said Cosine, enraged.

"Well, I believe you there too that he's bad-mannered. He keeps grazing all over the place. He even pinched me a little. Bit off a piece of me. But what you said about catching him – that I don't believe."

"Why?"

"He just left for botany. When he saw all the cabbage and iris there, he started braying happily and ran off as fast as he could. That saved my life, otherwise he would have grazed all of me," said Spot.

"Oh, what a relief," said Cosine and headed back to tell the others that he'd gotten rid of the wretch.

A partial circle fell into his arms as the hero of the day and he pretended not to notice her defects. So everyone was happy and content. It was enough reason to celebrate.

***

In the morning, Boss got to school first. She marched militarily, large, tall and always overdressed in layers of clothing with various sweaters and vests, regardless of the season.

Her enormous, strong hand grabbed the doorknob to the geometry classroom and almost pulled it out of its bearings. She opened the door with a victorious smile on her face, then stood frozen in place several moments before letting out a cry when she saw the same disorder that she found every morning.

"The little rowdies! How'd they get into the classroom, that I'd like to know. They're doing it on purpose, just to spite me," she grumbled as she picked up figures, rulers, triangles and chalk from the floor.

"An ambush... I'll lie in ambush, that's what I'll do! Hmm, I've done that... I've done that several times. I hid over there in the bushes in front of the school. The boxwood scratched me all over. Once I even tore my socks. I looked like a bag lady when I came out... And zilch! Hey, nothing! There was no one anywhere!

"You little wiseacres! Don't you try your sabotage on me! Lenka will catch you, or my name's not... Boss!

"Hmm... from the back! Yes. Why didn't I think of that before, the rowdies enter the back way from the school-yard! They jump over the wall and come in to make a mess," said Lenka as though delivering a speech, as she cleaned the geometry classroom, concocting a plan to catch the offenders.

***

Miss Symmetry opened the classroom door. Everything was in its place. The children stood up in an orderly manner to greet her.

"Sit, children. Today we will have a practice test that will give you an idea of what the final test will look like. Get your tools ready, put your notebooks in your bags. You will be given a test paper with the problems. Katarina, please hand them out to the left half, and you, Andrew, do the right half."

Then she unlocked her drawer with a well-guarded little key. As she took out the tests, a scrap of paper slipped out. She picked it up and was just about to throw it into the wastepaper basket when she saw that a message was written on it:

Your pretty face is in my dreams,
Waiting with the pastry shop's cream,
After fifth class come by this way,
For whipped cream pie to make your day.

The message was not signed. It was typed, so she couldn't use the handwriting to try and figure out who sent it.

The message had obviously been thrown in through the narrow space between the two locked drawers and was intended for her alone.

"Hmm, the pastry shop? Which pastry shop? There are two in the vicinity. Who could have sent it? Hmm. This seems most like my colleague Theodore Sage, but why would he write me a letter? He could simply invite me to have some cake and I would go. Hmm.

"If I could be certain he was the one, I would go. This way... Well... I won't go, but I'll watch from the other side of the street," she decided.

Andrew and Katarina looked at each other furtively with a grin in the corner of their mouths so no one would notice. Their plan was straightforward: orchestrate an "accidental" encounter between Pythagoras and Symmetry, but outside the classroom. And, of course, they would watch from a hidden place.

Mr. Pythagoras could barely wait for school to end so he could continue writing. The school year was coming to an end. A ball was being prepared for the graduating classes.

Everyone was thinking about what to wear, and he was thinking about her. Sofia. Miss Symmetry. Whatever he was doing, she was always before his eyes. The thought of the long summer vacation that everyone looked forward to made him uneasy. The thought that he wouldn't see her until September 1st made him uneasy.

This is why rushed to finish the book. He would print it in two copies. One for her, the other for himself. That way they would be together, regardless of where they were on the globe.

The second session children had left the classroom and Mr. Pythagoras was still struggling to put things away that kept falling on the floor.

That's when Boss the janitor entered the room.

"All they do is make a mess. That's how they've been taught. Afterward I put everything in order, as though I was the one who made the mess. I'd teach them all with a good spanking. Look, broken chalk, rulers, erasers. Just look at the blackboard! Well, I won't wipe the blackboard. The class monitors can wipe it tomorrow, that's what."

Boss grumbled as she cleaned and Theodore finally packed his things. He opened his drawer and saw a scrap of paper inside. Just as he was about to throw it away, he saw that Lenka had already emptied the wastepaper basket and was still grumbling. So it was a better idea not to provoke her with new garbage.

"I'll put the scrap of paper in my pocket and throw it away at home. Lenka here would gobble me up if I threw it away now, after she's cleaned the classroom," he whispered to himself. "But, something's written on it!"

He smoothed out the paper and saw:

Wait for me when the sun goes down,
At the sweetest corner in town,
Where various pies are in stock,
And whipped cream pie is in white blocks.

The message was clear, but he didn't know who had sent it. What terrified him most was looking ridiculous, since this had already happened even without such games.

"Hmm, the children are playing a game with me. But it might be her? Sofia! Maybe she's inviting me. I can't not go, but I can't go either. I'll walk along the other side of the street and watch whether anyone appears in front of the 'Sweet Secret' pastry shop," decided Theodore.

He had just finished a new chapter of his book about the final ball and was still under its impression. He wanted so much to share it with Sofia, but had firmly decided not to until the book was finished.

Chapter Three

THE BALL

When Sissy Sine Wave mentioned the graduation ball, general chaos and panic ensued. Indeed, the graduation ball was approaching, but only for those who were good, hard-working and successful. Everyone suddenly started touching up the traces of their injuries and jumping around as though the test had not just taken place and nothing terrible had happened. The clamor grew even louder as everyone tried to find the best partner for the ball.

A Diameter grabbed the hand of the first Circle he came across. A Radius had been hanging around her earlier, but when Diameter appeared he didn't say a word, not because he was scared but because a little farther away he'd seen a lonely, smaller circle and thought he might be able to pass as a diameter with her, which was certainly considered a higher function.

"Why should I be a radius when I can be a diameter," he said out loud and took the little circle by the hand, to her delight.

He turned to wave at the larger Circle and saw Straight Line standing over her. Diameter and Straight Line had already crossed swords and begun a merciless battle of life or death. They started dueling.

"I saw her first, and first come first served!" said Straight Line.

"I'm a better catch for such a gentle and round lady such as she. Who are you? An ordinary segment AOB. Don't you see how limited you are? I'm Mr. Right. My horizons are broader. She can get to know wide open space with me. And what can she do with an ordinary AOB segment? If you were at least a ray, we might be able to talk, but even then we wouldn't have anything to talk about. This way, you don't stand a chance against me."

The Circle just listened and didn't get involved. She was proud that two gentlemen were fighting over her. She fluttered her long eyelashes from time to time, fixed her hairdo and lipstick, and waited to fall into the winner's arms.

After a long battle, when Diameter saw he truly had no chance, he said:

"Alright, I'm going over to that big circle to be her chord. But remember, I'm only doing this because we're first cousins, otherwise I'd show you how I fight!"

The big circle was consoling a very little circle who had burst into tears.

"Don't cry, child, it happens to everyone. When you grow up you'll learn to take care of yourself."

"But Auntie, if I lost 2RPi then I'm no longer a circle. What's a circle without a circumference?"

"Calm down, who says you lost 2RPi? You just misplaced it somewhere. I keep telling young people to take care of their things and maintain order, since order is the basic Constituion of the land of Geometry."

"I don't know where it is. Here's my radius and diameter and PiR^2, but it's not there."

"Wait a minute, if the area's there, then so is the circumference!" concluded Auntie Circle.

"Oh, of course," said the little circle and stopped crying.

"If R is here and Pi is here, then everything's here. You're crying for nothing, you'll only smear your makeup. Just look at Diameter and Radius watching you cry. Go and fix your makeup and put a smile right back on your face," said Auntie Circle to her.

A little farther way calmly sat Angle Alfonso of 85 degrees and his sweetheart Elizabeth II of Complementary, better known as Bette. She was tiny, blond and very slender with barely five degrees at her waist. They were inseparable, always together, as connected as twins, and no one could stand between them. In Geometry they were like Romeo and Juliette.

A somewhat older couple was nearby, mustachioed Mr. De Gamma and his companion Mrs. Delta of Supplement. They were always a couple too, so there was no confusion this time either. They would attend the ball together as they had in earlier years. They were used to each other, but everyone knew they were a hopeless case, as noted by some tangents and chords.

Nevertheless, the greatest panic arose among those tangents, straight lines, CD segments and EF segments that has been removed from the problems as unnecessary.

The most tragic among them were a ray who wasn't sure whether she was a ray or a segment, and a circle who wasn't sure whether she was a circle, an ellipse or something similar. Some even commented that she was an ordinary curve trying to pass herself off as a geometric shape, but had been caught on time.

They searched through the so-called waste to see what could be used as a partner at the ball.

As they were digging around, a ray stretched out to lonely Cosine and attached to him to her delight and that of Sissy Sine Wave, and in the end it was seen to be to his delight too.

A very astute Miss Straight Line, tall and elegant, caught sight of Mr. Logarithm who was a foreigner and did not belong in their world, which was obvious at first glance. But Miss Straight Line was not a chauvinist. She had attended a course on tolerance and was not prejudiced against members of other fields, textbooks and school grades. She not only had no prejudices, she also had no choice.

"Better a foreigner than being alone," she whispered. He too was not bothered by the fact that she was considerably taller or rather longer than he.

When everyone had paired up, they put on their finest clothes, fixed their makeup and hair, and headed for the ball. They were just about to cross the threshold into the reception room when before them stood none other than He. Protractor Pro in a blue policeman's uniform.

"Stop! Where are you folks going?" he asked sternly.

When no one answered, he continued:

"My, my, what a nice fragrance! Are you going to some sort of celebration?"

They remained silent, knowing what awaited them. Now he would start to measure them and they would not be able to pair up as they wanted since someone would once again be unnecessary, and none of them wanted to be unnecessary. The ball was a matter of prestige.

After a long pause, Mr. Alfonso spoke up.

"We're going to the graduation ball. The final exam is over, so we thought..."

"The exam is over? And!? Did you pass the exam?" asked Pro.

"Yes, we did," replied a circle.

"Who asked you, fatty?" said Pro.

"I'm not fat, I'm full. A full circle! Look a little closer at my slender waist," she replied, offended.

"So, did you pass the exam?" repeated Pro, addressing Angle Alfonso.

"We passed. And the exam is over and we... I mean, passed. I suppose. We did."

"You did? Who are you to say, you angular teenager. Is there anyone here older than you?" asked Protractor Pro.

"There is, my uncle Mr. Da Gamma. He's bigger and older than I am," explained the young and slender Mr. Alfonso.

Mr. Da Gamma twirled his dark moustache and said:

"I have nothing to add or to take away. As my nephew, young Mr. Alfonso, said, we're going to the ball. My darling Delta and I got all fixed up for the occasion..."

"You don't say! You two fixed yourselves up. And you others? My, my! Look at how you paired up! Heaven forbid!

"And why are you so red, like you came from a battlefield?" noted Pro.

No one spoke. They'd been convinced no one would notice.

"We get like that after a test. We're a little winded," explained a ray.

"Time was short, so we hurried to finish," added a triangle.

"Well, you don't say! You get a little flushed after a test?" repeated Pro cynically.

"Yes, that's it. And it's a little from my cheeks," added a circle. "I put on a bit more rouge. You know, evening makeup."

"What a line you're feeding me," replied Pro distrustfully. "I wouldn't say it's from makeup. It's from a red pen! I'm not as stupid as you think!"

"Who's the muscle?" asked Logarithm from the side, holding his Straight Line's hand.

"Quiet, he'll see you're a foreigner, and he's strict. He'll send you away and I'll cry like rain. I'll be broken by sorrow and become a ray," she whispered through clenched teeth.

"Who's this guy? Who are you?" asked Protractor Pro. "Where'd you come from?"

"I am His Highness Logarithm. And I come from Higher Mathematics," he said proudly.

"You don't say. Your Highness?! This isn't a history text-book where we learn about kings and princes."

"I'm not from history. I'm young and handsome," replied Logarithm.

"Come again? Handsome? Your mama must have told you that," said Protractor Pro.

"Not my mother, but Concentric Circle Cindy told me I'm handsome. And she knows about beauty," said Logarithm from Higher Mathematics.

"Aha, Cindy! She knows about beauty," replied Pro. "I can see you're a foreigner. What are you doing here?"

"I don't know. When I woke up, I found myself here. And since I have a red sash across my chest, I'm probably a prince."

"Prince?" said the protractor in surprise.

"Yes. A prince or a duke," he said.

"Don't get carried away, that's not a sash. That's a red pen and it crossed you out. You're a mistake, dear boy!"

"Me, a mistake?! Watch what you say! I'm 'sir' to you! That's how to address me in future, since I'm from Higher Mathematics!"

"What a joke. I'm going to call that little calculator and see if something didn't fall out again when he took the exam. He must have lost you along the way, 'Sir'!"

Logarithm turned his head the other way, clearly very offended, as his Straight Line consoled him and brushed the dust off his lapels.

But Pro was unrelenting:

"So you want to go to the ball? Well, that's not possible."

"Why not? The exam's over," they all asked in unison.

"The exam's over? And did you pass the exam!? I asked, but no one's answered that question," he repeated.

"Well... well... we passed," they said rather unconvincingly.

"Aha, you passed the exam, you're red from rouge, and what's this... pardon my French... F doing at the end of the problem?"

They were all mystified and had no idea how it got there. Pro continued:

"See how red and full of life it is. And as big as a door! So? What's it doing there? Is this another mistake, like that 'princely sash'?"

They all bowed their heads in shame and listened without a word as Pro put them through the grinder.

"That's not an F!" piped up an inequality from some angle that no one had noticed before. "That's not an F on the exam, it's a function f that I lost. You know, I used to be an equality and ever since I lost that function I've been an inequality and, well, hiding around the angles. I'm so embarrassed," she explained and hid her face in her hands.

"You can imagine my shame. An inequality and here I am in Geometry where the law of symmetry reigns."

A little later she spoke to the function sternly:

"Come back, you vagabond! Where'd you run off to? You have no idea how much trouble you've caused me!"

The function f bowed its head and without a word returned to the inequality, turning her back into an equality, with a sigh of relief.

Protractor Pro just cleared his throat a little. He didn't like this. The others grinned, since this event had returned their hopes that everything would end well after all.

Then an Acute-Angled Triangle suddenly got an idea and climbed onto a horizontal tangent. He went up on his toes and shouted:

"A D! There's a D! I can see it!"

"Bravo!" shouted the others and looked at Pro pointedly.

"And not just a D but a D+!" added the Triangle, raising his hands in the air happily. He lost his balance and fell off the tangent, breaking into three parts.

Then he looked Pro straight in the eyes and before he could jump up and measure him, the triangle pulled himself together and returned to his original state.

Protractor Pro scratched his head and started measuring something on the side, as though preoccupied with important work, and the couples passed by him, happy that they deserved to go to the ball.

***

The children stampeded out of the classroom. By the time the bell stopped ringing, the classroom was empty except for Miss Symmetry. She closed the roll book, packed her things, and tried to open the drawer that Mr. Pythagoras always kept locked. She'd hoped it would be open again and she would find the manuscript of his book.

Ever since she'd sneaked a look at several paragraphs, she hadn't stopped thinking about him. Indeed, he was clumsy and muddle-headed, which might have made him endearing. His eyes radiated kindness and revealed a big heart full of love for geometry.

The school year was coming to an end. She knew that she would miss seeing him when the sessions changed.

The night before she had run into him going for a walk in front of the school. What a strange time to be walking in front of the school. He also found it interesting that she was taking a walk at the same time and same place.

They were both flustered and started stumbling over their words. Then Sofia got hold of herself and started talking about the problems he had prepared for the final exam. They both forgot why they had come to that same place at that same time, completely forgetting the pastry shop.

At one moment something started rustling in a bush not far from where they were standing. As they looked in that direction, the bush started to move. Before they thought to get away, Boss the janitor appeared before them.

"What's going on, what are you two scheming about? Hmm, there's something fishy going on here. That's what you teachers are like, you just join that union and organize strikes."

"What strikes, Lenka?" they asked in unison.

"Yes, yes. Strikes! All you think about is how to get out of working, just like these rowdies who only think of how to cut class. All you do, one and the other, is cause disorder. You make more of a mess than I can clean up," she grumbled from the bush.

Sofia and Theodore were embarrassed and didn't even try to deal with Lenka.

"I've got to go," said Sofia and went in one direction while he went in the other, even though it was the opposite direction from where he lived. He didn't want to follow Sofia because of Lenka, who would once again see something that didn't exist... even though he certainly wanted it to.

***

Night was the only free time Theodore used to write his book. It grew and developed more and more every day, even though time was running out and the end of the school year was near.

He and geometry had somehow grown close and come to understood each other a lot better. They had peered into each other's soul and seen what ordinary viewers did not. This is why Theodore was able to write a book about something that others could not even envisage, let alone live.

Chapter Four

NO GEOMETRY WITHOUT A SPONGE

It was a sunny day in June. Judging by the temperature, summer had begun. The bell rang at the end of the last class and the children left the classroom as quickly as possible. The geometry classroom was deserted almost instantaneously. That is, only the children deserted it, and once they were gone the classroom's permanent residents appeared onstage: numbers, equations, geometric shapes and figures.

So when the last student closed the door, a circle started rolling around the teacher's desk, enjoying the sun that fell directly on her through the open window. A block and two logarithms were sunbathing along with her. Then came Sine and Cosine and Mrs. Sine Wave, known as Sissy, who never let Sine go anywhere without her. Not far away a square root of four was lounging in the sun, clinging to a two squared.

"Darling, we're the perfect couple!" he whispered in her ear, while she pretended not to hear, although she didn't push him away.

When the old pyramid considered to be a few years younger than the Pyramid of Cheops came out into the sun, Protractor Pro let the triangles relax a little too, since he had kept them under strict surveillance and measured them all day long.

Each one found a place they felt was closest to the sun and basked. When the space was almost filled, She came. Concentric Circle Cindy. She looked around for a place to settle, but didn't see anything suitable without someone to be tangent to her, which she certainly would not allow.

She was holding her skirt of a thousand petticoats, marking time, as she tried to attract attention.

Mr. Sine saw her first. He would have loved to offer a place next to him, but he didn't dare utter a word, since Sissy was sitting behind his back. She was wearing sunglasses and underneath them kept an eye on what everyone was doing and whether anyone was looking and Mr. Sine. Everyone knew she was jealous so they stayed away from Mr. Sine, wanting to spare themselves from any awkward situation.

"Darling, can I go and buy us some ice cream?" Sine asked Sissy.

"Sit there and sunbathe. Cosine can go," she replied without moving.

Cosine pretended he hadn't heard, and might have tuned her out since she chattered and carped without letup.

"Come on, Cosine, spring to those lazy feet and bring three ice creams, or better yet three fruit cups with four scoops of ice cream and chocolate sauce. Did you get that?" she ordered.

Cosine got up reluctantly without a word and went to get refreshments. He passed close to Cindy who was still looking for a place in the sun, but he took no notice. His only worry was that someone might take his place next to Sine, since he had a title deed to that place bequeathed to him by his grandfather, Cosine the First. In the testament it said: "Safeguard your place under the sun next to Sine, since that is your patrimony".

Sissy Sine Wave was watching under her sunglasses, hoping Cindy would catch Cosine's eye and he would start following her, but nothing happened. Cindy wanted that too, but since a fruit cup was more in demand this time owing to the heat, Cindy started spinning on her tiptoes in order to attract attention.

As Cindy spun, she didn't notice that a dark cloud had covered the sky and rain was falling, accompanied by strong wind. A real summer storm. Carried by the wind, rain drenched the inside of the classroom through the wide open window.

Everyone started fleeing in panic to save themselves from the flood and wind. They hid on the pages of books, under notebooks, behind the vase with flowers. Some jumped into the half-open desk drawer. A ball fell to the floor and rolled to the opposite corner of the classroom, and a cone spun around on the floor until it found shelter under a school desk. Everyone found refuge somewhere except for Cindy who was in the same place, spinning in a circle on her tiptoes, and then a strong spray of rain drenched her completely.

Only then did Cindy realize what was happening to her. Only then did she see there was no one around her. The water was already so deep that Cindy started to sink. With her last breath she called out for help, but her cry went almost unheard from the screeching hinges on the window frame that was buffeted by the wind, slamming periodically against the wall.

Cindy waved her arms, trying to swim, but she was prevented by her skirt of a thousand circles that was already soaked with water and pulling her under. No one left their shelter since the storm was still raging. Another powerful burst of wind roared into the classroom, closing the window behind it, but Cindy was still struggling with the elements.

Spongy Sponge watched all of this from his shelf next to the blackboard, delighted with the rain. He hadn't been sunbathing because he didn't like the sun. On the contrary, he loved rain. The more rain the better, so he could splash around in it.

When Spongy saw Cindy drowning, he moved the board from the shelf, making something like a seesaw, and then asked Artemius, the large, older, dull-witted square standing on the shelf above his, to jump on the free end of the shelf.

Artemius Square looked down, afraid to jump into a freefall, but when he heard Cindy's cries for help, he jumped with all his might and weight onto the seesaw. This catapulted Spongy right onto the desk not far from Cindy. He soaked up the water in two or three gulps and Cindy was on dry footing again. Then his other end wiped the water drops from her petticoats and she was completely dry, but very exhausted.

The storm passed and the castaways began to come out of their shelters, shaking off the excess raindrops that Spongy immediately absorbed, not hiding his delight.

Everyone gathered around Cindy, realizing what had happened. Old Protractor Pro was the first to go up to Spongy and thank him, calling attention to his feat, which pleased the sponge immensely.

Then Pro went up to Cindy to measure her. First he measured her degrees. All 360 were accounted for. He measured her diameter and radius, they were there and so was circumference 2RPi.

"Oh, no!" shouted Pro. "Something's wrong! Let me see your area PiR^2! Cindy, your Ludolph has gone crazy! Do you know what it is? Pi equals 5.14! Cindy, you've got the flu! Of course, since you were heated up and then drenched. You have to go straight to bed."

Protractor Pro quickly made a bed out of blotting paper and put Cindy in it. A large circle brought Cindy some mint tea that she found in the flower vase.

Pro measured her Pi every half hour. The struggle to bring down her temperature was long and hard. They put compresses on her forehead and the soles of her feet. Of course, first they had to take off the ballet slippers that she always wore.

After a long battle, when Pi was once again 3.14, Pro sighed with relief. So did the others. Cindy was saved.

* * *

The silence was broken by the sound of a key unlocking the door and Miss Symmetry entered the classroom. All the inhabitants of the room kept quiet, as though nothing had happened. In a flash they all were in their places. The only one still on the desk was the sponge. Miss Symmetry closed the window that she had left open after the class and headed out. That's when she saw the sponge in the middle of the desk.

"What are you doing here?" she asked half-aloud. "Oh, those children. Someone left you in the wrong place again."

She picked up the sponge and squeezed it. A full puddle of rain dribbled onto the floor and she screamed.

"Oh, you children! How many times have I told you to leave the sponge on the shelf with the water squeezed out."

She picked up his shelf from the floor and put it back in place and then... and then Mr. Pythagoras opened the door and smiled. Miss Symmetry smiled too. She picked up her bag and headed out of the classroom.

"Excuse me for bothering you," said Mr. Pythagoras.

"You're never a bother. On the contrary."

"I forgot..."

"And I forgot to close the window."

"I forgot... I forgot what I forgot," he said and they both let out a laugh.

He didn't say anything special. He was flustered as usual.

They headed out the door. Before Mr. Pythagoras closed it, old Spongy blew a kiss to Cindy, so that no one else could see it.

She just fluttered her little eyes and sent him a gentle smile.

***

"Kids, to tell the truth, I feel sorry for the teacher," said Katarina. "He needs help."

"How can you help someone who trips over his own feet?" asked Andrew.

"He doesn't know how to dress. Have you seen his color combinations? I don't know how we can help him. No one's close enough to him to propose a new style," concluded Katarina.

"I think someone put the evil eye on him or some other hex," said Una. "There's no other way to explain such behavior and clumsiness."

"Why don't you sprinkle some of your invisible powder on him" added Andrew mockingly. "Or should we dip him in magic water. That might remove the hex? What do you say?"

Everyone laughed out loud. But Katarina was still thinking about how to help her teachers finally get together and reveal their feelings to each other.

Chapter Five

CONFLICT

They were all raptly listening to old Protractor Pro's heartfelt story, so no one noticed the monster approaching. Racy Eraser was sneaking up on them slowly from the bottom of the paper. She skillfully circumvented all the obstacles and resolutely advanced toward Cindy, threatening to erase her completely from the face of the paper.

The inhabitants of the land of Geometry were not afraid of old witches, dragons or bogeymen. They were not afraid of the dark either. Erasers were the greatest monstrosity for them. Some were peaceful and were there when needed, but this Racy Eraser was evil, wiping out everything that came her way.

This is why everyone screamed and ran for shelter. Sides, angles, tangents and chords flew about, degrees scattered and segments shattered. Geometric figures fled too, even old, sluggish Artemius, the wooden square who wandered about the classroom, looking for a place to hide. Chaos ensued.

Cindy looked all around, completely defenseless. The wicked eraser was getting closer, and just when she started erasing part of Cindy's petticoat, a very acute angle appeared wearing a cowboy hat. He stood before Racy and threw his hat into her gaping jaw, challenging her to a duel.

Without his hat, he was clearly not an acute angle but a handsome, young deltoid named Kite.

Racy Eraser was not prepared for a gentlemanly duel. She had only one goal – to erase Cindy's beautiful petticoat. She gasped and swallowed his hat. But, alas! His sheriff's badge stabbed her in the throat and Racy Eraser started to cough.

Kite grabbed the edge of Cindy's skirt and whirled her around as hard as he could. Cindy spun faster than she ever had before. She spun and spun and suddenly started to separate from the plane in which she was inscribed. She flew like a top or satellite above the plane. Everyone looked up and so did the eraser. Racy couldn't believe her eyes: the best bite had gotten away.

Conrad Compass stood to one side and shouted:

"Fly, Cindy, fly!" keeping his point directed at the eraser.

Racy Eraser looked at him and then turned toward the young deltoid Kite. Seeing he was in mortal danger, Kite made a pirouette on his acute angle and started flying like a real kite. He rose above the plane and flew to Cindy whose arms were stretched out to him.

It was a beautiful sight, like in a fairy tale. Cindy and Kite were holding hands and spinning as though they were dancing. Everyone watched from their shelters. Racy Eraser jumped several times, trying to catch them. When her attempts failed, she lay down and started rolling around the paper, leaving a dirty trail behind her. She screamed in frustration, since Cindy had been snatched almost out of her mouth.

Just then the classroom door opened and Miss Symmetry came in. She was stupefied at what she saw, unable to believe her eyes.

Cindy was floating above the plane. But she was no longer Circle Cindy but a true geometric figure. She had taken on a third dimension and become a real, true sphere.

A shadow was inscribed on the plane in the shape of a circle. Miss Symmetry put out her hand and Cindy dropped onto her palm. Next to her shadow was Kite's, who had also become a geometric body – a double pyramid. Miss Symmetry put out her other hand and he dropped onto her palm.

"I always maintained that you were the perfection of symmetry. Yes, yes! Now it's quite clear.

"The sphere and pyramid are part of the teaching material for sixth grade. That's the place for geometric figures," explained the teacher and placed them on the shelf among the other figures.

Cindy fluttered her eyes several times and Don Pyramidon kissed her hand.

"And you? What are you doing on the paper? Someone must have forgotten to put you back in their pencil case," she said to Racy Eraser, putting her in a wooden box and sliding the lid shut. Racy struggled and screamed but almost nothing was heard from the closed pencil case.

Miss Symmetry put the test papers in her drawer and then headed for the door. Before she left, her eyes met Conrad Compass's. He was saluting. She smiled.

As she left the classroom, the sounds of "The Blue Danube" waltz were heard. Before the door closed with a bang, Protractor Pro looked out and saw Mr. Pythagoras in the hallway waiting for Miss Symmetry with a smile and special sparkle in his eyes. But the door closed, the key clicked, and Pro gasped, then mumbled:

"Hmm, hmm, hmm... boy is he diligent. He's working in both sessions!"

But he didn't say a word to anyone. And who was there to tell, anyway. He was devoted to Miss Symmetry. Well, and to Mr. Pythagoras, but in the line of duty, while he was at her service for his personal gratification.

***

Pro could not get out of his head what he'd seen through the slightly opened door. He couldn't define his feelings, which ranged from ecstasy to jealousy. Unlike him, Mr. Pythagoras had accurately and precisely defined his feelings, but he didn't have the courage to say them out loud. He was waiting for the book to do it.

During this time, Sofia just smiled kindly and waited to see him in the classroom when the sessions changed. She told no one about her dreams and desires. She hoped that Theodore would muster the courage to ask her out at least for pastry, if not to the movies or dinner.

Chapter Six

MOONLIGHT

It was night. The whole school was sleeping, getting ready to greet the children in the morning, refreshed. The displays in the classrooms were sleeping blisssfully. But, the sounds of a waltz emanated from the geometry classroom and disturbed the sound of silence. Actually, they didn't disturb it. The music enriched the silence that did nothing to resist it. One might say the silence was pleased at having its emptiness filled.

The Moon was floating on a cloud, living it up. When it heard the sounds of a waltz, it stopped and peered through the window. It couldn't believe its eyes or ears. Pressing its nose against the school window, the Moon caught its breath. What a sight to see.

Sphere Cindy and her young Don Pyramidon were dancing on the shelf where the geometric figures were placed. At first only the two of them danced, while the others stared at them fixedly. A bit later, the other figures were carried away by magical sounds of the waltz and a real, true geometry ball began. Everyone swayed and even the shelf started swaying to the rhythm.

Those who knew how to dance were joined by those with two left feet. A trippy trapezoid was dancing with a little circle and trampled her pretty little shoe. She let out of cry of alarm.

"Excuse me!" he said, and she straightened her petticoat. She might have looked a little like an ellipse, but it was not very noticeable in the dark.

The entire classroom was dancing, but no one was as talented as Sphere Cindy. She had a feeling for rhythm and her perfect symmetry could be seen to its full measure. She spun in a circle as Don Pyramidon towered over her, holding onto her smooth figure, gliding with her as though on ice.

Everyone was having a great time. So was the Moon, so much so that it decided to sprinkle a handful of silver on them. Silver fell all over the classroom, but mostly on Sphere Cindy, making a veil that fluttered with her around the silver dance floor.

Old Square Artemius was so carried away by the rhythm that his weight almost knocked down the shelf, threatening to send the figures toppling to the floor. But the leading couple was no longer on the shelf. They were dancing on a platform made of moonlight. The Moon danced too, embracing the nearest star, swaying on the cloud.

The dance lasted until dawn. The Moon almost forgot to leave and was reminded by the Sun as it entered through another window. When no one took notice, the Sun cleared its throat a little. The Moon started and quickly gathered its sprinkled silver, waved to everyone, winked and sailed off behind the cloud.

Sphere Cindy and her Don Pyramidon were back on their shelf. Cindy was all aflutter with the sparkling silver veil the Moon had given her that night and forgotten to take away in its haste.

The only noise was a low hubbub and whispering as the figures exchanged their impressions of the ball. The classroom door opened and Miss Symmetry entered. She went up to the shelf with the figures. They were all in their places and were just a little winded from dancing all night long.

Cindy and Don Pyramidon had their arms around each other. Next to them stood a small cone. It was round like Cindy and tall like Don Pyramidon. The teacher smiled, picked up the little cone and put it on her palm, then kissed it.

"Little beauty. Perfection!" she said.

Cindy and Don Pyramidon watched on proudly, and when the teacher left the classroom, Cindy laid her head on his shoulder.

Protractor Pro quickly went up on his toes before the classroom door slammed shut, wanting to see... Actually he wanted not to see Mr. Pythagoras and his smile and sparkling eyes when Miss Symmetry appeared.

The door closed with no sight of the teacher. It was a weight off his mind, but not for long. The weight fell on his foot and he yowled several times, so he didn't hear quite clearly to whom Miss Symmetry was talking so amiably, almost chirping, behind the closed door.

"Serves you right," said Ellie Ellipse, laughing out loud. Racy Eraser laughed too inside her wooden pencil case, although she didn't know what she was laughing about.

"Quiet over there, or I'll measure you!" said Pro sternly.

"You can't do anything to me anymore," said Ellie. "I retired long ago so I couldn't care less if you measure me or not."

"Listen, you know that I train karate and have a blue belt," said Pro sharply.

"And I've been training 'I don't care' for a long time. And I already have a 'that'll be the day' belt!" she said and continued laughing at the top of her lungs.

"Oh, those women," whispered Pro to himself and looked out the window, as though not at all interested in what she had to say.

* * *

Protractor Pro did not sleep day or night. Sometimes he napped, but quickly jerked awake, rubbed his eyes and hastened to make sure everything was under control.

He looked out the window and caught sight of Miss Sofia and Mr. Theodore walking off together toward the large park. He pulled the curtain over the window and pretended he hadn't seen anything. He believed he had Sofia's favor and that she appreciated his years of fidelity.

Nevertheless, what he had just seen undermined his tranquility.

Theodore was radiantly happy to finally be in Sofia's company. His excitement prevented him from thinking of an intelligent topic of conversation. He didn't have a lot of experience in this regard and everything that came to mind seemed unsuitable or even ludicrous. But keeping silent was not suitable either.

"Miss Sofia..."

"Sofia. Please just call me Sofia," she said, making things a lot easier for him.

"Of course. And please call me Theodore."

"Thank you, Theodore," she said with a smile.

"Sofia is a pretty name. It's Greek and means 'wise'. Just like my last name, Sage."

"There, we have that in common," she added.

"And we also have love in common."

"Love?" she said in surprise.

"Yes. I mean love... of geometry," he said, thinking fast.

"Yes, of course. Geometry is my great love. That's why they call me Symmetry," she said with a laugh.

"And me Pythagoras. But I don't mind. It could have been worse. They might have called me Obtuse."

"Haha! They might have. Children find the best nickname for everyone. It's enough to hear the nickname to know the person's characteristics."

"That's true. See what nice cubes these are. Symmetrical," said Theodore, indicating the whipped cream pie in a pastry shop window.

"Hmm, I don't think they're cubes. I'm sure they don't have the same sides. They're quadrangular."

"Cubes."

"Quadrangular."

"Let's measure them," he proposed.

"Let's," she agreed and they went inside the pastry shop.

"Please give us a portion each of whipped cream pie and a tape measure," she said to the pastry shop owner.

"We don't serve tape measures in the pastry shop," he replied. "You have to bring your own."

"I don't need a tape measure, my whipped cream pie is quadrangular. You can see that with the naked eye," said Sofia.

"Try mine, it's a cube," replied Theodore, offering Sofia a spoonful of his pie.

"Mmm, I think yours is sweeter," she remarked.

"Because it's a cube. Cubes have their charms," said Theodore. "I really love cubes. They're pretty because... because..."

"Because?" she asked.

"Because of the symmetry," he said, looking her in the eyes. They smiled and took each other's hands across the table.

This did not escape the sharp eyes of Andrew and Katarina who were in the same pastry shop, accidentally or on purpose, buying ice cream. They smiled and winked at each other, pretending not to notice the teachers, who didn't notice them. They were too preoccupied with each other.

Chapter Seven

SANDY CIRCLE

Sandy Circle was Cindy Circle's first cousin from Mošorin. Even though Sandy always thought she and Cindy were as similar as siblings, the others in Geometry weren't of the same mind. Particularly not Cindy. Indeed, their mothers resembled each other like two peas in a pod, but Cindy always said about herself that she was pretty after her mother, while Sandy was... pretty after her father.

So, while Cindy was always the center of attention, Sandy would roll after her as clumsily as if her radiuses were quarreling.

Those who knew what was going on in Geometry, or rather those who knew things that no one else knew, maintained that Sandy Circle had fallen into pear juice, or rather juice had been spilled over part of her, so one of her radiuses had shrunk a little. When Sandy rolled, this was why she dragged a bit to the left toward Mošorin, and ever since then resembled a pear more than a circle. Some wicked tongues whispered that she was no longer a circle, that both her 2RPi and PiR^2 were out of order, but no one mentioned it out loud, because she was Cindy's first cousin after all, and Cindy would burst out crying if anyone from her family was declared an ellipse or, heaven forbid, something that had no name or had wandered in from biology, zoology or some other place.

One event which, from a different angle, might be called an incident, happened while Sandy was rolling after Cindy. Her slightly shortened radius constantly lagged behind the one that had not been bathed in juice, and Sandy started losing control of her course. She struggled with herself and these two quarreling radiuses. When she reached the edge of the desk, she let out a scream and the very next moment landed on the floor.

A hush fell, and a few seconds later everyone was looking for Protractor Pro who was in charge of such incidents.

Pro was aware of the difficulty of his task. He straightened his uniform, twirled his moustache and went down on the floor to look for Sandy. When he got down there he had quite a sight. Lying on the floor was just a curved line with an irregular shape.

"Oh, no!" said Pro. "Poor Sandy, who's going to patch you up? Tell Conrad Compass to come here at once. And throw down the lasso! And scotch tape!"

"Why do you need the lasso?" they cried in unison. "You're not going to catch wild horses, are you?"

"I just might! If I catch up to them. Hurry it up."

They tossed down the lasso, he threw it and – lo and behold! He caught one of the runaway radiuses. It was the shorter one. But after being drenched in juice it could no longer be used.

"What am I to do?" wailed Pro and clutched his head. Then he said:

"Shhhh!"

And all the others said:

"Shhhh!"

Pro twirled the lasso and walked stealthily toward a flower pot. He threw it out with all his might and caught the other radius – the longer one.

The radius screamed, struggled and called for help, all in vain.

"I don't want to be a radius! I want to be a freelance artist! I'm a born actor!"

"You don't say. And what part can you play since you're so thin?" said Pro.

"I can play the part of a diameter!"

"Hmm!" said Pro. "You're no fool! One diameter is like two radiuses. Stand there and don't move!"

Pro took the scotch tape and taped him to the desk leg.

Then he looked around.

"I have 2R... Not bad. There's still hope that I can give Sandy back her circumference. But, where's Pi? Can anyone see where he's hiding? There's no circumference without him!"

During this time Pi was running like a comet with his long tail of 136 decimals. He was running at the speed of light, but nothing could escape the sharp eye of Protractor Pro. He knew that Sandy could not live without Pi. He twirled the lasso and caught his long tail.

The tug of war lasted till noon and even after noon. Pi almost reached a mouse hole, intending to hide so he didn't have to be part of the play where he had the role of a component of a circle's circumference. Pro pulled once more with all his might and the long tail broke off so that after the three and the point only the one and the four were left.

"Woe is me! My beautiful long tail," wept Pi. Pro took the scotch tape and before Pi realized what was happening, taped him to the one playing 2R.

Conrad Compass quickly turned around his axis and – lo and behold, a miracle!

Sandy Circle was once again standing before them. With 2R and with Pi... with two decimals, but believe me, no one noticed. She was much smaller, but like new. She got up off the floor, straightened her petticoat and kissed Pro.

He smoothed his moustache and said:

"Sandy, you look so much like your first cousin, it's as though you're not from Mošorin. Why didn't I notice that before?"

Sandy fluttered her eyelashes. She had always wanted to hear that. And he, the old fox, seemed to know that.

***

Theodore was waiting for Sofia after fifth class, which once again did not escape Protractor Pro's sharp eye.

"Sofia, you were right yesterday. The whipped cream pie was quadrangular after all, just as you noted. Give me a chance to level the score."

"Hmm. That would be fair. What is it this time?" she replied.

"*Žerbo* cubes. The other pastry shop has layered *žerbo* cubes with chocolate frosting. Let's check whether they're faking it or they truly are cubes. Our students often go there and they shouldn't learn the wrong thing. If we establish that they aren't cubes, we'll request they change the name," he said.

"Theodore, I think we have to take action! And not only *žerbo* cubes – don't forget mint chocolate ice cubes, petit fours, cream cake and who knows what else," she replied, smiling broadly.

He smiled too and they headed for the pastry shop.

Chapter Eight

PI

Sunday morning dawned, sunny and quiet. Birdsong could be heard through the open window as the sun's warm rays caressed the inhabitants of Geometry, announcing that it was time to wake up.

Of course, the first to wake up was General Protractor Pro. He washed his face with cold water, smoothed his moustache and began his morning inspection.

When the others heard his decisive steps, they all jumped lightly to their feet and stood at attention.

But something strange happened this morning.

"Hmm, hmm!" said Pro. "I don't like this."

Everyone had gotten up except the circles, cylinders and cones.

"Something's wrong here. Is it some kind of virus? Did they catch cold? But why just them? Why didn't a single triangle catch cold? Even Obtusest is here, the most obtuse of all the triangles," said Pro, thinking out loud.

"Let me do a little measuring so we can see what's to be done," he continued.

He went up to the first circle lying without moving. She didn't lift her head. Pro examined her and measured her, then measured another and another.

"Well, folks, I've reached a diagnosis!"

"Is it an epidemic?" asked an acute-angled triangle.

"You might say, but you don't have to worry. You're pretty immune. Folks, the circles have fallen sick because of a lack of Pi!"

"Piiii?

"Pi!"

"Piiii?"

"Pi! Does anyone know where he's hiding? Or shall I go look for him?"

"General, General!" interjected Sissy. "The window was left open. Did he run off?"

"As far as I understand," said Logarithm, "Pi has never been a geometric figure. He's an ordinary number."

"Actually, he's not so ordinary," said Sissy.

"Hmm," said Pro.

"But he's always been Ludolph's and not yours. Maybe he went to see Ludolph," said Christy Chord.

"Yes, maybe Ludolph found him and took him home," said Sissy.

"Does anyone know where Ludolph lives?" asked Christy Chord.

"Oh, my goodness!" shouted Pro. "That's all I need. I can see they're missing something. They've lost their circumference and area. What kind of circle has no circumference and area? No kind at all. They aren't circles anymore.

"It's true that Pi is Ludolph's number, but he was so calm, quiet and stable. That's why we called him a constant. Now what can I do? Where can I find one like him? Where?

There are no others like him. There is only one Pi, 3.14 with his long tail of 136 decimals.

"Oh Pi, Pi, what have you done?" wailed Pro.

"Who said Pi, Pi?" interjected dusty old Artemius Square who was on the highest shelf in the classroom, almost forgotten. He had the best view up there, but since he was very old he often napped during the day, while he couldn't sleep very well at night.

"I said Pi," repeated Pro.

"Were you thinking of our Pi?"

"Do you know any other Pi?"

"I don't know any other. You know, I can't sleep well at night, I have rheumatism. Once long ago when I was a young Square, I got caught in the rain."

"We know that story. You fell into a bucket of water and it gave you rheumatism," added Sissy.

"Yes, yes, I didn't get caught in the rain, I fell into a bucket of water, and before that I got caught in the rain."

"Alright, spit it out. You couldn't sleep, and...?" said Pro.

"Well, that's when I got rheumatism, and it reacts to the weather, so I couldn't sleep, so I... forgot what I wanted to say," said Artemius.

"So why did you ask about Pi?" continued Pro.

"Well, as I said, I can't sleep because of my rheumatism, I thought it would rain and here it is a sunny morning, but there will probably be a downpour in the afternoon..."

"So what happened with Pi?" asked Pro, visibly irritated.

"Like I said, a sunny morning and Miss Symmetry left the window open..."

"That's when you saw her. You weren't napping then?" mumbled Pro.

"I was napping, but the squeaky window woke me up. That building superintendent's always napping. He can't find the time to lubricate the hinges on the windows so they don't wake me up," said Artemius.

"Alright, Artemius, are we going to hear something about Pi?" said Pro angrily.

"Pi?" asked the Square.

"Pi!" replied Pro.

"Pi is Ludolph's number and it's 3.14... 3.14... I forget the decimals that come after."

"That's not important, but did you see Pi somewhere from that high position of yours?"

"Pi?"

"Pi, of course!"

"Well, I saw him," replied the old Square. "You don't have to shout! I'm not deaf! Everyone thinks I'm deaf, since I'm old, and all I have is rheumatism!

"And that Pi of yours, let me tell you, the window was left open and the sun was shining and rain is expected, and that's when the fish are biting, and he heard that Theodore Sage was going fishing."

"Whooo?" asked the others in unison.

"Theodore Sage," replied Artemius the old Square.

"Who's that?" wondered Protractor Pro.

"The geometry teacher, Mr. Pythagoras!" they said in chorus.

"Oh, yes, Mr. Pythagoras has a first and last name," laughed Pro.

"Yes, he does," continued Artemius Square. "As I said, Mr. Pythagoras was going fishing and this morning before sun-rise he took his fishing pole and there he is on the school's lake, but I don't know if he's caught anything. He's using bleak for bait, I think, although I can't see that well, but my hearing's great so you don't have to shout."

"So what if Mr. Pythagoras uses bleak for bait?" asked Pro angrily.

"He could use worms or bread," replied Artemius.

"What does that have to do with Pi?" shouted Pro.

"Nothing at all," replied Artemius.

"So why are you wasting our time? We're looking for Pi so we can save the circles," said Pro.

"That's what I'm saying. Mr. Pythagoras is using bleak for bait and Pi is sitting next to him, and they're probably chatting about geometry," said Artemius.

"Ouf," sighed Pro with relief. "Give the circles some water. He'll probably come back soon."

Not long after, Pi appeared at the window. He entered the classroom slowly, quietly, quieter than when he'd left to go fishing. There were no fish in his bucket, but his boots were full of water. He sneaked over to Spongy Sponge and took off his boots there, hoping that no one had seen him.

But the watch that Pro had put in place, $2R$ and R^2, jumped right into his arms.

In an instant the circles received a circumference and area, as Pro scowled at Pi.

"The fisherman's shorts are wet, nothing for dinner did he get!" said Pro angrily.

"I thought, if the teacher can…" mumbled Pi.

"You're not a teacher. When you're a teacher then you can go fishing too, now get to work!" said Pro sternly.

"No, I'm not a teacher. That's why I didn't catch anything, but he did and he took it to Miss Symmetry…"

"Hmm, hmm. Well... Everyone to your places!" ordered Pro and sighed deeply, seeing that Theodore's imagination had started working.

***

Someone rang Sofia's doorbell. She opened the door and found Theodore in rubber boots and fishing tackle. He was holding a large carp.

"Theodore, did you buy a fish?"

"I caught it. Can't you see my equipment? It's Sunday and sometimes I fish on the lake on Sunday. If you allow me, I'll prepare it myself."

"What a wonderful idea, particularly since we've been picking on the pastry shops. Thank you, Theodore. Put the fish in the bathtub and we'll have it for dinner. We can eat outside in the garden," she said.

Theodore couldn't wipe the smile off his face. He put the carp in the bathtub, but kissed it first.

Then he sat on a wicker chair in the garden.

"Do you drink coffee?"

"No, thank you, I don't. My grandmother used to say that children grow a tail if they drink coffee."

"Haha! I remember, they told me that too. But you're not a child."

"I'm not... I suppose. Although I'm not quite sure. But I do like café latte."

Sofia brought café latte and little vanilla cookies with apricot jam that she had made herself.

"Please help yourself," she said.

Theodore tried one and said:

"The cookies are wonderful!"

"Go ahead, I have a whole bowl full," she replied with a laugh. "You know that poem:

Little round vanilla cookies
Boys and girls adore these goodies,
I'll make hundreds in my pans,
And fill them with apricot jam.

Haha, cute little poem."

While they were making dinner, Theodore peeled the potatoes and cut them into triangles, squares, circles, trapezoids...

And Sofia peeled the carrots and cut them into circles, triangles, squares... When they put their bowls together, they both laughed out loud.

No one knows what happened afterward, since night fell. And we really would like to know.

Chapter Nine

LENKA THE CLAIRVOYANT

Obtusest, an old, faded obtuse triangle, was dozing in a notebook, its pages yellowed with age. Sometimes when he woke up and stirred, he would make sure that everything was in place. As soon as he saw that angles Alpha, Beta and Gamma were there, and his sides were accounted for, he would smile with satisfaction. Before he dozed off again, Obtusest would look proudly at the bottom of the page where he was drawn. There in the bottom right-hand corner was written a big fat A in bright red. Under it was written in neat handwriting "Miss Symmetry." It was the signature of the geometry teacher beloved by all, even Obtusest, although he'd never told that to anyone.

Obtusest was proud of his A and considered it a great success, particularly for an obtuse-angled triangle like he was. For many years before him not a single of his relatives had received an A! He was especially proud of the signature under the A. But don't tell a soul.

So Obtusest dozed off again. He fell asleep as soon as he closed his eyes. He dreamed that someone was pecking at him, tugging him lightly and tickling him, and in the end that a mustachioed monster tried to devour his obtuse angle Alpha.

"Get away from my obtuse angle!" said Obtusest in his dream. "Why don't you try Gamma? Huh? You don't dare because he's too acute! Just three degrees and twelve minutes! You found an Alpha, so fat and sluggish, to nibble on!"

But the monster paid no attention to his words. Perhaps because nothing is heard or understood in dreams unless they are subtitled.

The monster became more and more aggressive and Obtusest started fighting in his dream. He worked up a sweat, panting hard. When the monster broke off a piece of Angle Alpha, Obtusest woke up. He collected his angles, trembling with fear. Before him stood that mustachioed monster from his dream.

Obtusest had no idea how something from his dream had ended up on a yellowed notebook page, perhaps because he was obtuse, or maybe there was another reason. Be that as it may, the monster was there, staring at Obtusest with wide open ugly eyes.

"Who are you? Who said you could eat my obtuse Angle Alpha?"

The monster didn't reply and continued nibbling Angle Alpha, approaching Beta from the back.

When the monster bit off a larger piece, Sine and Cosine jumped off Angle Alpha. Obtusest didn't even know that they existed, and neither did the monster, who spat out the piece of angle, took several steps back, turned around and ran off, looking back to see if anyone was in pursuit.

"Thank you, first cousin!" said Obtusest to Sine.

"Thank you, too," he said to Cosine. "Who are you two? I didn't know you were here. Why didn't you get in touch earlier, we could have played tic-tac-toe to pass the time."

"We are functions and we don't play tic-tac-toe," replied Sine.

"Oh, sorry. Functionaries. I can see you're some sort of big wigs, since you're wearing ties. I'm Obtusest from third grade. Almost everyone knows me. And where did that monster come from?" he asked.

"That's a bookworm. Nibbler. He's a real nuisance. This notebook hasn't been touched in a few years, so he moved in. Books and notebooks should be shaken out from time to time. There, two janitors just entered to clean the classroom, dust the books and wash the windows," replied Cosine.

Just when Cosine said the word "shaken", a real tremor began. Actually, it was a trembling notebook.

"It's not another test, is it?" cried Obtusest. "It always shook like that before a test!"

"Just so it's not recycling!" piped up Angle Gamma perceptively.

"What's recycling?" asked Obtusest.

"What do you care since you can't change anything," said Sissy Sine Wave.

"Excuse me, ma'am! My respects!" added Obtusest and fell silent.

Bright sunlight was shining down on Obtusest and all the others who were by him, around him or in him at that moment. He rubbed his eyes and shaded them with his hand so he could make out what was happening. There was a hush, and then a strong thud.

"That one's perfect! Old ones are the best," said a voice on the side.

"That's right. It'll absorb everything," said another voice.

Then a wet, black cloud descended on Obtusest and the others. It was pitch black and there was no air. Everything resounded as though they were under a bell. They wandered about in the darkness, arms outstretched, crying, sniffing the air. No one knew what had happened.

And then Sissy Sine Wave shouted:

"Eureka!"

And everyone fell silent.

"What's that you say, ma'am, did a eureka attack us?" asked Obtusest.

"Stop talking nonsense," said Acutely Supplement, who was always there, making sure that Obtusest didn't do anything foolish, but without Obtusest's knowledge. Actually, Obtusest was the only who didn't know, unlike all the others.

"You've got an acute wit," noted Obtusest.

"The more obtuse you are, the acuter is my wit," he replied.

"Please stop, gentlemen, that smell... it's coffee!" concluded Sissy.

"Coffee?"

"Coffee," she insisted.

"Coffee?"

"Coffee! Once, against my will, I found myself on a napkin in a café. First they drew a sine wave, that's to say, me. There were some other numbers there too. They were checking problems from the test. And then I smelled coffee. Just like now."

"You never informed me that you frequented cafés," said Sine of Angle Alpha from somewhere in the dark.

"I said I was in a café 'against my will'," repeated Sissy Sine Wave. "And you and I didn't even know each other then."

"Hmm, and might I ask who was your function sine?" said Sine.

"Well... it was... that's not the subject right now. Let's get back to this dangerous situation," said Sissy, collecting her wits.

Just then the light came back and Sissy sighed with relief.

"Someone turned off the darkness," said Obtusest.

They rubbed their eyes and looked around. What a sight there was to see. There was a new circle on the paper where they were drawn, symmetrical and with a rather large diameter. But it had not been drawn with a compass. They'd never seen anything like it before.

"Is it from Mars?" asked Angle Beta.

"Definitely. It looks like it was made by a space ship," said Christy Chord.

"Come on, as though that's important, can't you see it's pressing down on me?" said Angle Beta. "Move it, lift it up so I can get out from under it!"

They all ran up to help. They lifted, pushed, begged it to move, without success. Poor Angle Beta remained lying under it.

Women's voices were heard once again:

"My dear, this notebook is great!"

"Like I said, these old notebooks absorb the best. But don't take too long, we have to clean the classroom. Tell me, what do my coffee grounds say?"

"Well, my dear, there's a tall blond man. He's thinking of you."

"Mmm, it's not..."

"I wouldn't say it's him. This one parts his hair on the other side."

"Who could it be?"

"Press the grounds to see if the wish will come true."

"I don't know, but it's not him. In addition, I hear he's taken."

"Taken? Since when?"

"Since he's started taking his colleague, Miss Symmetry, to pasty shops."

"Oh!"

"Oh, oh! People say they went to all the pastry shops until they found a cake that had the same sides."

"Why is that important for a cake?"

"I guess because of the symmetry. That's something from that... from that geometry."

"Come on, press the grounds."

"Uh oh! The cup still hasn't drained."

"Turn it over here on a clean page, let it drain real well. Old notebooks are the best for that, when Lenka says so."

***

Theodore was almost finished with the book. The school year was drawing to a close. Just a few more days and the children would be happy, and he would be sad because Sofia was going to her parents' house in a small town. Indeed, he would be going to his parents' house in his own small town, but if she were to stay here, he would stay too without a second thought.

"Hello, Sofia. What are you doing tonight?" asked Theodore, feeling more relaxed since they were on a first name basis.

"I'm reading a book about geometry. About Tales and Pythagoras... sorry. I didn't mean anything bad."

"It's alright. I know they call me that, I think we already mentioned it. The name impresses me. They call the biology teacher 'Seal' and the chemistry teacher 'Cyanic Acid'. I got off easy."

"Hahaha!" they both had a good loud laugh.

"But I have to look at a digital book."

"Hmm, digital. That's something new. I'd like to look at it too, but I wanted to go see a movie tonight. If you want, you can, I mean, actually, I wanted..."

"Excuse me, Pythagoras put it succinctly: 'Do not say a little in many words, but a great deal in few!'"

"Sofia, come with me to the movies!" he said at last, mustering his courage.

"What movie are we going to see?"

"It has an unusual name: 'Point'!"

"How interesting. A lot can be said about it," she replied.

Chapter Ten

POINT

Cindy Circle had always considered herself the most important geometric shape since time immemorial.

"Hmm," said Segment AB. "If you were number one, the whole world would be round and wavy. But just look at these pretty streets and squares, straight as an arrow. They're all segments. Some are longer AB, some CD, EF, but they are nevertheless all segments."

"Can I say something?" asked little, barely visible Point in a soft voice.

"No, you can't. You're an ordinary Point. What can you have to say about this vital issue," said Straight Line. She turned toward Segment and continued.

"It's no good when you're limited. You can be longer or shorter, but you're still finite. Essence lies in infinity, my dear truncated soul."

"If essence lies in infinity, then you can't find any fault with me," noted Inclined Plane.

"Can I say something?" repeated Point.

"Move aside a bit so you don't get hurt. You're no match for such conversations," said big old Artemius Square, who then addressed the others.

"Don't get on my nerves! Where's your third dimension? You're just ordinary shapes."

"I wouldn't be putting on such airs if I was as fat as you are!" replied Straight Line.

"Excuse me? Who's fat? Are you insulting me?!" said Artemius angrily.

"No, I'm just stating the obvious," replied Straight Line.

"Well, here's something to remember me by. I'm going to turn you into two rays and a bunch of small, finite segments, and you'll stop all this tomfoolery and talking about infinity!"

He jumped down from his shelf among the geometric shapes. An uproar ensued of the kind never heard of, even before a typhoon-test engulfed Geometry.

There was thunder and lightning, segments and straight lines were shattered, diameters, volumes, angles and degrees went flying. Squares became rhomboids, pentagrams became triangles, straight lines broke into two rays. Some ellipses were rolling around that had been circles beforehand.

The battle lasted longer than a typhoon-test with five problems, each with a, b, c. It was the greatest battle recorded in the history of the land of Geometry. It stopped when no one was left moving on the battlefield. Some cries and moans were heard, but no one was left intact.

That's when Point spoke up from behind a bush.

"Can I say something?" asked Point again.

She repeated it a little while later.

"Can I say something?"

"No, you can't. What can you say, so tiny and insignificant, at such an important and serious historical moment as this?" said Artemius Square, who was severely injured.

"Look around, do you see my volume anywhere? It seems I lost her in the battle."

"She's nowhere to be seen or maybe I don't see well, since I'm too small. You already came to that conclusion," noted Point.

"Come on, sister..."

"Since when am I your sister?" asked Point.

"Well, maybe not my sibling, but a first cousin, since you've been messing around here in geometry," said Artemius. "Just look around, if you see my volume tell her that I asked her to come back to me, because without her... without her..."

Artemius burst into tears.

"Don't cry. She'll come back. Who needs so much volume... except you."

"No, she won't. She won't come back. They're like that. When they leave, they never come back. She might find another," said Artemius.

"Okay, I promise I'll give her your message if I run into her," said Point. "But only if you let me say something."

"Alright, say it and stop pestering," replied Artemius.

"I wanted to tell you, I'm Point."

"Bravo, you're Point and full stop," answered a broken triangle.

"There is no Geometry without me," continued Point.

"Quiet, please. Someone will hear you and think you're wrong in the head," said Straight Line who was no longer a straight line but a ray, although she still wasn't aware of this fact owing to battle shock.

"There's no Geometry without you?! Hahaha!" laughed Artemius Square.

"There's no great Geometry without you?! Who needs you when you're so small? Scram and don't come back! You're a whit, a jot!" screamed Ellie Ellipse, grabbing a tangent and throwing it at Point.

Point moved out of the way so she wouldn't get hurt and then started crying. She took her rucksack and headed for the coast. She sat in a boat and started rowing toward the open sea.

"Why should I stay here when no one understands me? I'll go to a desert island since no one needs me."

When Point left the land, the real problems began. The inhabitants of Geometry started to disappear. They simply dissolved. Some thought an epidemic had resulted from the battle, some thought it was the end of the world, and then He appeared. Protractor Pro in person.

He was wearing a general's uniform. He had a thermometer in one hand and a jug of water in the other. He went onto the battlefield and treated the injuries.

"Tsk, tsk, tsk," said Pro disapprovingly. "What's happened to poor Geometry?! I always said, be prepared for a typhoon-test, but it never occurred to me that you'd have a civil war and overthrow the Theorem. Just look at you, you'd overthrow axioms as well as theorems. Papa Pythagoras is certainly turning over in his grave. Poor thing. Who's going to patch you up now and restore order?

What's this? *The square of the length of the hypotenuse equals the speed of light passing through the square root of the carrot...*

"Goodness me! Botany and physics mixed in with Pythagoras' theorem.

"I can't help you by myself. I have to ask my colleagues for help, Conrad Compass and Rupert Ruler. Maybe if we work together we can stop the catastrophe."

When Conrad Compass and Rupert Ruler arrived, they grabbed their heads:

"Uh-oh!" they chimed together in displeasure.

"We have to save what we can. Look, over there's a circle who's all drawn out. She's neither a circle nor an ellipse. Let's inscribe her again," proposed Conrad Compass.

Protractor Pro and Rupert Ruler lifted up the circle and Conrad Compass got ready to inscribe her again, but he couldn't find the center point.

"Hurry up," said Pro. "She's heavy. We can't hold her up like this forever."

"I can't find the center point. It seems to have disappeared," said Conrad Compass.

"Point?" whispered someone from the crowd.

"Point, what else. What's Geometry without points," added Compass.

"She's gone. That stupid Artemius Square chased her away," whispered someone.

"How can there be no Point. How can there be Geometry without points?" said Conrad in amazement.

"What?" shouted Pro. "Aren't you aware that you all come from Point?!"

"How can I come from a tiny, ordinary little point?" announced Artemius, who was still looking for his volume on the battlefield, rummaging through geometric bodies and broken shapes.

"How? Now you'll see how, since you've expelled her. You've been seized by an epidemic of nonexistencitis!

Without Point you don't exist! Do you understand?! You are all composed of countless points," explained Pro.

"Oh, I lost point A and point B. Now I don't know whether I'm a segment or something else. I don't know where my end B is and my beginning A, since there are no initial points," said Segment AB.

"You're missing just the end and the beginning?" asked Rupert Ruler.

"You, my dear, don't exist. You are composed of countless points," Pro said to her.

"And me?" interjected Straight Line.

"You too, of course," confirmed Rupert Ruler.

"How can that be when I'm longer than Segment AB. If she has countless points, then I must have two or three countless points," she concluded.

"Stop speculating!" shouted Pro, taking off his cap and wiping the sweat off his brow.

"Point! Where is Point?!" he shouted at the top of his lungs.

Silence ensued.

"I asked, where is Point?"

"Well..."

"Well?" he asked thunderously.

"Well, she went out into the wide world," whispered one of the wounded.

"What?" shouted Pro.

"Into the wide world, the narrow darkness," added someone else.

"She wouldn't leave just like that! What did you do to her?" Pro roared with anger.

"Nothing. She's so small and insignificant. What could we do to her?"

"Insignificant, you say?"

"Since she's so small she can't be significant like me, for example," said Straight Line.

"Can't be stupid like you! Don't you know that you are composed of countless points?!"

"I know, but that one doesn't matter, more or less," replied Straight Line.

"But she's not an ordinary point. She's a Notion! If she disappears, Geometry disappears!" bellowed Pro.

"While you bicker, you will all disappear off the face of the land of Geometry. We have to bring Point back to the land of Geometry, since it cannot exist without points.

"A statue should be raised to her on the central square!" said Pro, still shouting. "You've ruined everything! Just look! Geometry is no more. It has fallen apart. It does not exist! Oh, how naïve I was. I didn't realize you were unaware of what's fundamental!"

As he said this, Miss Symmetry and Mr. Pythagoras entered the classroom. He placed an unusually large box-like quadrangle on the desk. She put a smaller object next it that that resembled nothing they'd ever seen before.

The teachers gazed at the new arrivals happily, then held hands and left.

* * *

Pro was the only one to notice that the teachers were holding hands. All the others were looking at the strange device that had been left on the teacher's desk. No one dared approach. It was larger than any of them.

They examined it, in spite of their injuries, but came to no conclusions.

"General, say something!" said Rupert Ruler.

Pro flinched. His head was still filled with the image of the amorous teachers holding hands.

"He's found his footing, I'd say," said Pro, thinking of Mr. Pythagoras.

"Who?" asked Rupert.

"No, no! I was just lost in thought. But what's that on the desk?" he asked, greatly surprised.

Chapter Eleven

COMPUTER

"A mouse! A mouse!" shouted a circle, lifting her long skirt as she tried to climb onto a block lying there.

"A mouse!" shouted the others, looking for the nearest shelter.

"Calm down! Quiet! What's all the noise about?" said Pro, stepping in.

"A mouse!" screamed Tina Tangent. "Look at how big it is! I've never seen a mouse like that before! So big and so strange."

Pro turned toward where they were all staring and had quite a sight. Indeed, an enormous mouse was standing on the edge of the desk.

But it wasn't an ordinary mouse. No, no. Pro had run into various mice, moths, bugs, and spiders that liked to get into old student notebooks and gnaw their insides, destroying the geometric shapes. Once some mischievous mice almost ate up an old cylinder, thinking he was a wheel of cheese. He's still full of holes today and had to be retired.

But this time it seemed to be a very serious matter. Pro had never seen a mouse like this before and things did not bode well. He straightened his uniform, put on his cap and stepped before the guest, ready to lay down his life for his homeland.

"Hmm, hmm! Do we have here an unannounced guest?" he asked, while the others waited in silence for events to develop.

But the mouse was silent and said not a word. Pro repeated his question, and when he didn't get an answer, he was joined by Conrad Compass and Rupert Ruler. The chalk and even Racy Eraser came to help, fearing the worst.

They went up to the mouse and slowly let down their guard. Pro even touched it.

"This mouse is not alive!" he shouted.

As soon as he said this, the mouse moved. They took a step back and found shelter behind big old Spongy Sponge, then started to devise a defense plan.

Just at that moment Mr. Pythagoras and Miss Symmetry entered the classroom and put another large quadrangular object on the desk, standing on its thin edge.

Now there was a computer, in person. The inhabitants of the land of Geometry realized that a great change was on the horizon. Some panicked, thinking it was the end of the world, some were speechless, some cried, and then Computer spoke:

"Dear friends. There is no reason for fear. Geometry has always been the most orderly and precise land on earth. It will remain so. A new era has arrived. Geometry will continue to exist, even more precise and modern than ever before. The computer will be your new home. We are writing a new chapter of history. Without fear and panic, the mouse will copy you and place you in your new home where there will be perfect order."

Pro felt he should be the first to sacrifice himself. So he stood bravely before the mouse.

"I'm sorry, but I have to disappoint you", said Computer. "Only geometric shapes and figures will go into the computer. We are grateful to you, Protractor. You have finished your active life honorably and earned your retirement. Congratulations, enjoy it in good health and cheer."

Pro could not believe it. A tear streamed down his face and he tried to hide it. The others were sad as well. They immediately forgave him for all his criticism, all his unnecessary measurements and remarks.

"Will I be the prettiest and most important one there as well?" asked Concentric Circle Cindy.

"No, Point will be the most important. It has been that way up to now and will continue in the new computer era. Everything is composed of countless tiny points."

Cindy didn't like this answer, but agreed nevertheless to move to New Geometry. Suddenly she was in the middle of the screen. She started twirling this way and that, spinning around, and it must be said that she liked it. When they saw how much fun Cindy was having, the others entered their new home without a second thought.

Protractor Pro, Rupert Ruler, Conrad Compass, Racy Eraser, Spongy Sponge, Chalk and Blackboard stayed in the classroom. They waved to each other.

Rudolf Ruler was fortunate that Miss Symmetry had put him in her purse. Some considered it an accident or luck, but he considered it a privilege.

"Computer is right! It's time to retire!" said Rupert Ruler, climbing onto the shelf. The others followed him. Only Pro grumbled:

"Just when I almost succeeded in measuring the square of a circle! This very moment. They're doing this to me on purpose."

He looked at Mr. Pythagoras quite sternly, and then gazed at Miss Symmetry.

She had put a sign above the shelf: *Museum Pieces*. She opened the door to the classroom and on the plate that said: *Mathematics Teachers*: Miss Sofia, she added a last name – Sage. Under it was written: and Mr. Theodore Sage.

"Sofia is a Greek word and means – wise. Now you are wise squared," said Theodore in jest. "I'd like to give you a book."

"A book? A collection of math problems with their solutions?" she said in delight.

"No, this is a fairy tale."

"Haven't I outgrown them?"

"We have to keep the inner child alive so we can continue. The child is father to the man... so said a wise man long ago."

"This is *A Tale of Geometry*. I wrote it for you."

"But who would write a fairy tale about geometry?"

"Someone who loves geometry... and a geometry teacher," replied Theodore.

Then he took a book out of his bag. Geometric figures "smiled" from the cover. At the top was written:

PYTHAGORAS' PHANTASMAGORY
By Theodore Sage

He opened it to the first empty page and wrote:

To my dear Sofia
From her Theodore.

Sofia kissed him. Silence reigned for several moments and then from the shelf came a hubbub, agitation, and even whistles, after which the shelf with its museum display pieces broke. Whether out of jealousy or joy, it has yet to be established.

The display pieces fell and scattered about the floor, just like after a dangerous exam.

But no one was upset. Theodore touched the mouse and clicked. Point appeared on the screen and waved at them.

Then music started and the two teachers danced to the "Blue Danube" waltz.

About the Author

Olivera Olja Jelkic, a children's author, has been writing and publishing for 25 years. She has published more than 20 novels. She has been a member of the European Academy of Sciences, Arts and Literature in Paris since 2018. She is the winner of the "Golden Badge" of the Cultural and Educational Association of Serbia for her contribution to culture and promotion of culture and books. She is an honorary doctor of science from the Slobomir P University; the creator and owner of the project "Little Free Libraries". Oral narrator, where she reads and records books at the Association of the Blind, which are published in an audio version adapted for the blind.

Her books have been translated and published in several foreign languages: English, Slovenian, Chinese, Russian, Uzbek, Macedonian, Ruthenian, Hungarian.

Olivera's novels can be divided into two groups: fiction for younger children and novels for older children, which deal with serious topics such as: child trafficking, attitudes towards pets, problems of transgender people, legal problems, and similar.

She has won a number of awards for individual novels, some of which have been named Book of the Year. Recently, she has also won several awards for her entire oeuvre, both in Serbia and in the countries of the region.

Contents

Olivera Jelkic
A TALE OF GEOMETRY

London, 2024

Publisher
Globland Books
27 Old Gloucester Street
London, WC1N 3AX
United Kingdom
www.globlandbooks.com
info@globlandbooks.com